Shades of Raven

Eureka in Love Series

Tamara Hart Heiner

Also by Tamara Hart Heiner:
Perilous (WiDo Publishing 2010)
Altercation (WiDo Publishing 2012)
Deliverer (Tamark Books 2014)
Priceless (WiDo Publishing 2016)
Vendetta (Tamark Books 2018)

Goddess of Fate:
Inevitable (Tamark Books 2013)
Entranced (Tamark Books 2017)
Coercion (Tamark Books 2019)
Destined (Tamark Books 2019)

Kellam High:
Lay Me Down (Tamark Books 2016)
Reaching Kylee (Tamark Books 2016)

The Extraordinarily Ordinary Life of Cassandra Jones:
Walker Wildcats Year 1: Age 10 (Tamark Books 2015)
Walker Wildcats Year 2: Age 11 (Tamark Books 2016)
Southwest Cougars Year 1: Age 12 (Tamark Books 2017)
Southwest Cougars Year 2: Age 13 (Tamark Books 2018)
Southwest Cougars Year 3: Age 14 (Tamark Books 2019)

Tornado Warning (Dancing Lemur Press 2014)

Shades of
RAVEN

AMBER

"No! Raven! How many times do I have to tell you not to lick the cars?"

Amber fought back a cry of frustration as her two-year-old daughter proceeded to wipe her fingers across the wet mark she had left on the neighboring vehicle, dragging streaks of slobber over the red finish. Amber fished through the carpet bag she called a purse until she found a wet wipe, and then she cleaned Raven's face and hands. "Clarissa!"

Clarissa, who doubled as both the babysitter and one of Amber's only friends, hopped out of the passenger seat with a freshly applied coat of lipstick and a guilty expression on her face. "Sorry! Just had to freshen up."

Why would Clarissa have to freshen up? This wasn't her wedding. She wasn't even a part of the professional team here to make sure the wedding ran smoothly. Unlike Amber, who was one of the assistant managers to Tying the Knot and whose job was on the line if anything fell apart.

Like having her toddler clinging to her legs throughout the ceremony.

Amber took a deep breath and told herself to hold it together. It wasn't ideal, having Raven here at the wedding, but Amber's landlord had called her that morning to tell her she would need to be out of her apartment for four hours while her yearly pest control guy fumigated the condos for roaches and spiders. The landlord had only given her a twenty-minute notice, which meant Clarissa could not watch Raven at Amber's house like she usually did. And since Clarissa lived with five other girls whose characters Amber had not evaluated, she didn't want her to watch Raven at Clarissa's house.

Just be grateful Clarissa was willing to come to the wedding and watch Raven here, Amber told herself.

But being grateful and being pleased were two different things.

Amber scooped Raven up into her arms, trying not to wrinkle her silk blouse. Raven patted Amber's cheeks with her chubby fingers and then pressed a slobbery kiss to her mom's face.

"Wuv you, Mommy," she said.

Amber softened and squeezed the dark-haired child a little tighter.

"Now you mind Miss Clarissa," Amber said, panning Raven off to the babysitter as they neared the entrance to the hotel. Several granite steps paved the way to a sculpture of a crescent moon. "Do not do anything naughty."

"Otay, Mommy," Raven said, offering a sweet smile full of tiny baby teeth.

"You're not fooling anyone," Amber said, ruffling Raven's hair. Amber, of all people, knew how those teeth could bite.

"Where should we go?" Clarissa asked.

Amber turned slightly from the parking lot to survey the

turn-of-the-century hotel that loomed in front of them. A good majority of the weddings she planned were held at the Crescent Hotel, a famous landmark in the Arkansas Ozarks. But it wasn't childproof, and the banisters inside could prove dangerous. "Take her around back. There are some nice walking paths, a pretty garden. Keep her outside."

"Come on, baby girl, let's go play." Clarissa put Raven down on the concrete and took her hand, and the two of them walked away around the building.

Amber let out a breath as she watched them go, then turned to examine her reflection in the window of a delivery truck parked in front of the hotel. She questioned now the way she had pinned up one side of her straight, dark brown hair. With the turquoise frames on the edge of her nose, she looked more like a twelve-year-old girl that a professional wedding planner.

Even if she was only one of two assistants.

Her heart gave a little thump at the thought. The previous manager had moved to San Francisco, and Violet, the owner of Tying the Knot, would be on hand, evaluating Amber's performance to see if she was ready to take on the responsibility of manager.

Amber wanted the promotion. She yearned for it.

Violet would also be evaluating Ava, Amber's coworker.

The thought had Amber's stomach clenching tighter, and she pushed the turquoise frames a little higher on her nose. Ava didn't have a little girl to support. She didn't need the additional income the way Amber did.

Amber flattened her skirt and let out a deep breath. It was show time.

She headed straight to the banquet hall where the reception would be held. Her heels clicked smartly on the tile floor as she went around the corner. Even after half a dozen weddings behind her at this venue, she couldn't help admiring the ornate molding and carved pillars that decorated the room.

Not that the craftsmen had always done a great job. Several door frames were placed on the wall so crookedly that even Amber could tell they were off-center.

The banquet hall had been furnished with table rounds. Several hotel workers stood by the back wall carefully centering a long, thick oak table for the wedding party.

"Amber!" Ava came clattering over, tottering in her shoes, wearing a slimming gray dress whose simplicity spoke of sophistication. Her blond curls had been pinned up, but a few fell around her face. She looked like a wedding planner, and Amber fought back her worry.

"It's about time you got here," Ava said, her tone bossy and commanding. "I need you to go to concierge and ask for three more tablecloths. The ones they gave us are stained."

Seriously? Amber raised an eyebrow. She wasn't here to be a gopher. She'd graduated from that job months ago. "Just send one of the hotel employees."

Ava huffed and gave her a patronizing look. "I've got them otherwise engaged. You can do this." She patted Amber's arm. "I have faith in you."

Now Amber really did feel twelve years old, and being treated like a second grader didn't help. Arguing wouldn't help her case either, so Amber swallowed her pride and turned on her heel.

Ava's been doing this longer, Amber tried to comfort herself as she strode down the hall toward the front desk. Amber had only been with the company for six months as opposed to Ava's nine. And until recently, Amber had always been assisting Violet, learning the ropes instead of managing on her own.

Oh. The anxiety ratcheted up another notch. Violet would be arriving soon, and all she would see was Ava putting the reception together by herself. Had Ava planned it that way intentionally?

Amber walked with clipped, precise steps past the tall fireplace mantle and the sitting room in the lobby until she reached the check-in desk. Two employees stood there, though the pretty black-haired girl appeared to be distressed.

"It's not a big deal," the man said, placing a hand on her shoulder. "You'll get it right next time."

She nodded and blinked her large brown eyes.

Amber cleared her throat. "Excuse me," she said, leaning forward to catch the man's attention behind the counter. "I'm looking for someone from concierge."

He looked away from the girl and gave her a distracted smile. "Yes, I'll be with you in just a moment."

A high-pitched shriek behind her startled Amber, and she swiveled to see Raven racing past on the patio outside. Amber stiffened. If Violet caught wind of the fact she'd brought her child to the job site, it would be the end. She glanced around in a panic, wondering where she could hide, but just then Clarissa intervened, hooking Raven around the waist before the child burst into the lobby.

"Ma'm?"

Amber turned to see the young man looking at her, a professional smile in place underneath light hazel eyes.

"If you'll come with me, please?" He came out from behind the check-in desk and led her across the lobby.

"Thank you," Amber said, following him to the executive desk. "I'm working on the Hernandez wedding." She cast one last look toward Clarissa and Raven. They were seated at an outside table now, and Clarissa had dug out paper and crayons from somewhere.

The man followed her gaze and then looked back at her. "Are they disturbing you?"

"Oh no. No, that's not it." Amber glanced back and gave a sigh of relief that Raven was sitting quietly. Then she turned back to the clerk as he sat down behind the executive desk. "Yes."

"Yes?" He lifted an eyebrow, and Amber couldn't help noticing the way his brows framed his face, giving the impression of someone who was just high-browed enough to sit in first-class on the Titanic. And yet something about the quirk of his lips when he looked at her also said he would fit in just fine with the Irish in third class, doing a fancy jig to a harmonica.

She had completely forgotten what they were talking about.

Out of the corner of her eye, she saw Clarissa take Raven's hand and move her out of view. Amber exhaled and blinked at him.

"You needed to see concierge," he supplied.

Right. The tablecloths. "Yes. Where is that?"

He gave a head bow. "That would be me. I'm the hotel manager, which means I double for concierge, clerk, just about everything except the plumber. Sometimes even that."

"Oh, well, great. I'm glad I found you. I need three more round tablecloths for the Hernandez wedding. It starts in two hours, and I would like these tables done in the next ten minutes."

"Of course. You're the wedding planner?"

She nodded. One of them, anyway.

"I'll have them brought to you. You go and finish whatever you're working on."

"Thank you," Amber said, patting the top of the desk with the palm of her hand. She hoped he would follow through; finding dependable employees at each venue always made her job easier.

Which, she decided as she walked down to the banquet room and found it in chaos, would only really matter if she still had a job after today.

Ava stood by the back wall screaming at the two men who only moments before had been setting up the long table. On the ground between them lay shattered pieces of glass.

Amber took a deep breath. Her hand reached up automatically to clutch the angel charm on her necklace, and the motion soothed her. No wedding ever went smoothly, but it was her job to make sure the bride never felt the stress. She pushed her way forward. "What happened here?"

Ava pressed her palm to her forehead, a vein throbbing on her temple. "They dropped the centerpiece. The crystal bowl is broken. That was the one the bride specifically requested because it reminded her of her grandmother's bowl."

"It's all right." Amber turned to the man, who looked shaken and apologetic beside Ava. "Get a broom and clean it up. I'll find another centerpiece." The one advantage she had over Ava was that while Ava caved under pressure, Amber became stronger.

It was how she had survived the past three years.

The man nodded and scurried away, and Amber turned to Ava.

"Concierge is bringing the tablecloths. I have another crystal bowl in my car." She always brought the family heirloom to the weddings, just in case she needed it.

Ava opened her mouth to say something, but Amber continued before she could interrupt. "I know it won't be the same one, but that one is broken and shattered on the ground. So we'll use a different one. I'll get it. Take a few deep breaths. It's going to be okay."

With that, Amber walked away, confidence replacing her earlier doubt. Violet had to give this job to her.

TYSON

Three round tables.

No, three round tablecloths.

Tyson unlocked the cupboard containing the extra linens and stood in front of them. Towels. Bed sheets. Napkins. Why was he having a hard time remembering what she'd said? Probably because he spent too much time looking at her mouth instead of listening to her.

How unprofessional.

Three round tablecloths. Tyson grabbed five just in case. You never knew what might happen in a wedding.

Tyson had seen all kinds of things.

She was cute, with a kind of, girl-from-half-a-decade-ago look. Her short bob had only emphasized her slender neck, and something about the turquoise glasses made her seem fun and spontaneous and intelligent at the same time.

Tyson tucked the cloths under his arm and walked down the hall toward the reception room. He had seen her before, but this was the first time she'd ever spoken to him. She'd probably end up yelling at him before the day was over. Most wedding planners did.

Was it just him, or was it hot in here? He checked the thermostat on the main floor. It said sixty-seven, but outside the late July sun was pushing a hundred, so maybe the old system was struggling.

Or maybe it was just him.

He didn't see her when he stepped into the reception hall. Instead, a tall blond in a pencil skirt stood giving orders. Her hair was rolled up in a fancy bun, but from the furrow of her brow and the pinch of her mouth, it didn't look like things were going well.

"Tablecloths," Tyson said, lifting his offering.

The girl turned, her eyes narrowing in on him. "Go ahead and set them up on those tables there."

"Sure." Help check in guests, clean bathrooms when needed, set up tables for weddings. All things he hadn't known would be part of the job description when he took on the position of hotel manager.

And he'd had such aspirations for greatness when he was a kid.

The reception hall door swung open again, and he looked over his shoulder just in time to see the other girl walk in. Her heels clicked across the marble floor, and she carried in her arms a box nearly as big as she was. Tyson jumped up and hurried to her side.

"I can carry that for you."

She gave him a strange look and resisted when he tried to take the box. "I can do it."

"Sure, but that doesn't mean you should." He tried again to relieve her of it, but she didn't let go, so he gave up on the tug-of-war, letting her have it.

She moved away from him with the box and set it on the long table in the back. "Did you bring the tablecloths?"

She remembered him, at least. "I've already set them on the tables. I hope they were the right ones."

"There were only three tables without cloths, so as long as you didn't double up, I'm sure you got it right."

Snarky. Tyson bit back a grin. "Glad to know it. Anything else I can help you with?"

She had opened the large box and was slowly removing a crystal bowl. "Thank you, I'll let you know if we need anything more." She turned and looked at the blond. "Ava, I need you to message the bride and let her know what happened."

"Wouldn't it be better to not say anything? She might not even notice."

"She might not," the girl agreed. "Or she might. And then she'll think we tried to pull one over on her." She arched an eyebrow.

Her coworker looked flustered, and Tyson tried to figure out how he could re-insert himself in this conversation. "Sorry, what did you say your name was?"

She turned and blinked as if she had forgotten he was there. "I'm Amber Morris, the wedding planner." She held her hand out.

"Assistant wedding planner," Ava said, stepping to Amber's side. "We're both ranked the same."

Amber tilted her head. Even though she had to look up at the blond, her expression was definitely condescending. "We work together. There are no ranks." Tyson sensed there was more she wanted to say, but instead she looked back at him, forcing a smile. "Sorry we hadn't been officially introduced."

He gripped her hand firmly in his, surprised at the strength of her handshake. "That's okay. I've seen you here doing weddings. Just let me know anytime I can help."

"Thank you." She withdrew her hand and faced her coworker. "If you're not comfortable messaging the bride, I can do it."

"I'm perfectly capable," Ava said with just the right amount of fluster and indignation.

He was in the way here. Tyson backed out of the room, hoping Ms. Morris would need his help sooner rather than later.

AMBER

Raven's crying woke Amber early Monday morning. She picked up her phone and looked at the time. Almost five. Amber groaned and grabbed the pillow, pulling it over her face.

The crying didn't stop. "Go back to sleep, Raven," Amber whispered.

Like that desperate plea had ever worked. Days of stressful assignments coupled with sleepless nights had often left Amber feeling frazzled and half-witted. At least she had managed to graduate college before Raven was born. Not that she looked dignified or graceful waddling up to accept her diploma while eight months pregnant.

Consequences for her actions. And even though it had been a horribly bitter time in her life, Amber thanked the stars above that she only had to rely on her parents for minimal help before graduation. As soon as she landed a job with a salary, she moved out and put Raven in daycare.

She kept the lights off as she entered Raven's bedroom and moved to the toddler bed. Raven had not actually woken, but lay whimpering and crying on her blankets. Amber scooped her into her arms and settled back into the La-Z-Boy she'd put in the nursery for exactly this purpose. Raven's tiny body curled around her, the head of soft dark curls tickling Amber's neck. Amber cooed gently as she cradled her little girl, and though the exhaustion did not disappear, her annoyance at waking up early faded.

The weight of the angel charm hang against Amber's breastbone, and she touched the necklace. Her mom had given it to her when Raven was born. A reminder that with all the difficult times ahead, she had an angel in her life. Currently bottled into the feisty, rambunctious body of a toddler.

Yes, the months after discovering she was pregnant and would soon be a single mother had been harrowing and emotionally draining. But she wouldn't take it back for all the world.

Amber parked her car at the business plaza next to the trolley stop off of Van Buren. She glanced once at the awning hanging overhead proclaiming the wedding planning business, Tying the Knot, in beautiful pinks and whites and blacks. Then she let herself in.

The door chimed as she did so, and Violet poked her head out of the back office, wearing her signature wire frames connected to a chain around her neck, a warm and welcoming smile on her face. It didn't diminish when she saw Amber.

"Come on back. Let's talk about this upcoming garden wedding."

Amber followed Violet into the back room, racking her brain to remember the details of that particular wedding. Oh yes, the Hansen party. The bride wanted a destination wedding to Hawaii, but neither of the families could afford to take the whole wedding party out there. So instead they opted for the glass chapel in Eureka Springs but with enough flowers inside to make it feel like they had landed in the tropics.

Hawaii might be cheaper.

"I've scoped out a few flower shops in the area," Amber said, settling down across from Violet at the desk. "What we're looking at is on a much larger scale than they usually provide. I was thinking I could go out to Fayetteville. They're used to doing grand events."

Violet waved her concerns away. "We are as capable here. Just have to think outside the box. Why don't we try Connor Landscaping? They're local, and I don't think we've been taking advantage of their resources."

Amber pulled her notepad from her satchel and jotted down the information. "Do they do weddings?"

"Brandon does yards. Houses. He knows flowers, and he's been doing this a long time. I'm sure his company can help with our exotic needs." Violet winked. "You'll have to talk to his wife, though, because Brandon doesn't like to talk to women." She chuckled.

This could be awkward. "Can I get a list of the bride's must-haves?"

"Yes, but keep in mind the bride is not the professional here. If Brandon recommends something, I want you to bring it back as an idea. Our goal is to make the bride happy, even if it's in ways she doesn't expect."

Amber nodded, pressing her lips together to suppress a smile. She already knew this. Violet expressed the sentiment to her at least once every time they met to discuss weddings. It was safe to say it had been drilled into Amber's mind. "All right. I'll meet with the gardener and see what plans he comes up with." She hesitated, afraid bringing up her coworker would appear amateur, but then she shook it off. This was purely business. "Will Ava be working with me?"

Violet shook her head. "You're both doing a fine job, but I'm not using your talents to the best of their abilities if I have you working together. I've put Ava on the Bartlett wedding. You will be managing your own separate weddings and assisting on the others. I feel like that's a fairer way for me to evaluate you. Because, as we saw at the last wedding, I can't have two people in charge."

Amber grimaced. It was unfortunate Violet arrived in time to see Amber and Ava arguing over who should call the bride. She considered defending herself but knew Violet didn't really want to discuss who was right or wrong.

"No, I get it," Violet said. "Both of you are vying for the same position. It makes it hard to be civil at times. So I'm making it easier on you and just separating your duties. Got it?"

"Got it," Amber said. Violet was giving her the chance to showcase her leadership skills and abilities. Amber straightened her shoulders. She was very good at what she did, fastidious with planning and organizing. She would wow Violet with this wedding and prove she was the best one for the job.

Twenty minutes later Amber parked her car in front of a quiet old rambler with a sprawling yard around it. A work truck with the words "Connor Landscaping" parked in the gravel driveway. She admired the flowering bushes and hedges around the house, though Amber herself didn't have much knowledge about foliage and fauna.

The front door opened before Amber even got there, and a tall, aging gentleman sporting silvery hair and suspenders stepped out. His cornflower blue eyes crinkled into a timid smile when he saw her.

"You must be Mr. Connor," Amber said, smiling brightly and extending a hand.

Mr. Connor nodded. "Come on in." He turned around without another word and stepped into the house.

"Did you offer her a cup of coffee?" A woman with red glasses and purple hair came out of the kitchen, drying a mug in her hands. "Just because Violet's making you help doesn't mean you can't be social."

"Yes, Myrtle," Mr. Connor said. "Young lady, would you like a cup of coffee?"

"That sounds lovely." The sticky July heat was already making Amber's glasses slide down her nose, and she shoved them back up. She would really prefer a glass of ice-cold lemonade.

Mr. Connor disappeared into the kitchen around the corner, and Myrtle followed him. Her chiding voice carried from within, but Amber couldn't make out the words. She settled down on the floral-pattern Victorian couch and spread the papers from her portfolio across the coffee table.

"Here we are." Mr. Connor returned with two steaming mugs. Amber accepted one, though she didn't feel inclined to chug the hot drink in this weather.

But Mr. Connor didn't say anything else, and Amber took a few sips. Then she set the mug down and cleared her throat. "Did Violet tell you about the wedding?"

He nodded. "I looked over the file she sent me."

Myrtle appeared again in the doorway. "Show her your landscapes."

Amber leaned forward and listened with interest as Mr. Connor opened a photo album and pointed out different landscapes he had done.

Myrtle joined them on the couch. "Something like this might work for the bride. Or this." She tapped a finger to her lip. "But you know who would be great at this is my great niece, Lilly. She's even helped Brandon with several of these."

Amber nodded. "Uh-huh."

"We don't want to overwhelm her—" Mr. Connor began, but Myrtle cut him off with a wave of her hand.

"She might have just moved here, but she's sharp as a tack."

Mr. Connor didn't look convinced. "I'll talk to her."

Amber worried about getting too many fingers involved, especially when they hadn't been vetted. "What's her background?"

"She used to work in a flower shop," Myrtle answered. "She'll know which flowers are used for weddings. She can help with picking statement pieces."

It just might work. Amber would test the waters and see how well they worked together. She smoothed her hands down her skirt. "Can you put together an image of what you think you could do?" She wasn't sure if she should direct her question at Mr. Connor or his wife, so she included both of them. "Then I can take it back to the bride for her approval."

"Sure he can," Myrtle answered. "He can pick up samples from the greenhouse if she wants to see anything first."

Amber opened her mouth to speak just as her phone rang. She recognized the ringtone as that of Raven's daycare, and whatever she'd been about to say left her mind. "Excuse me just a moment."

While Mr. Connor put his photos back into the album, Amber stepped outside and answered the phone. "Hello?"

"Hi, is this Ms. Morris?" the young daycare worker asked.

"Yes," Amber said, dreading what was coming next.

"Raven has a fever again. You're going to need to come get her."

Amber closed her eyes. This was the second time in a week she'd had to get Raven from the daycare. "There's nothing wrong with her," she said. "I get her home and the fever breaks. She's not sick."

"I'm sorry, but it's our policy—"

"I know," Amber interrupted, her words clipped. Policy be damned. She would lose her job if this continued. "I'll be there in half an hour." That would give her time to wrap up this meeting with Mr. Connor. She'd go back to the apartment with Raven and do what she could from there. She had to get things done before her mom got into town because her mom had booked a ghost tour for them that evening. If Amber was lucky, she could still count this as a full day of work.

If she was lucky.

Mr. Connor looked up from the coffee table as Amber came back in. He lifted a bushy eyebrow. "Is everything okay?"

She must have looked flustered. "I'm fine. Just family things. It's time for me to head out. I'll be in touch."

"More coffee?" Myrtle asked.

"No, thank you. But I look forward to talking with you both again." She removed a business card and handed it to Mr. Connor. "As soon as you have some kind of layout, you can email it to me. How long do you think that will be?"

Mr. Connor stood and shrugged, putting the card in the front pocket of his pants. "Not long."

"By tomorrow afternoon," Myrtle supplied. "I'll make sure he talks to Lilly by then."

That was sooner than Amber expected. "Great. I'll keep an eye open."

She let herself into her car and focused her thoughts on the task ahead. Get Raven from the daycare and figure out what was causing these fevers.

TYSON

Mondays. The daily grind at the Crescent Hotel. It was a constant flow of people checking in and checking out, or going to breakfast, or trying to find a way into the salon, or signing up for the evening ghost tours.

"How's it going?" he asked Kevin and Jaya as he unlocked the office before lunch. He'd spent the past hour trying—and failing—to diagnose a light problem in room 404. Now he'd have to call an electrician and file paperwork with the new owners. They had bought it the year before, but Mr. Draper didn't seem to know what to do with it now that his wife had died. He kept cutting corners instead of fixing the problem, and it showed on the hotel.

"No issues," Kevin said.

"There's some lady on the fourth floor who says she's being haunted by Michael's ghost."

"Michael doesn't haunt the fourth floor," Tyson said automatically before realizing the absurdity of his statement.

But Jaya didn't react. She just nodded, the curly black ringlets bobbing around her ebony skin. "Yeah, you tell her that."

"Is she angry about it or pleased?"

"Hard to say. Just go talk to her and figure out what she

wants."

"On it."

The phone rang, and since Tyson was standing right there, he answered it. "Crescent Hotel, how can I direct your call?"

"I want one of your haunted rooms. And all the champagne in the hotel. For tonight."

Tyson rolled his eyes. Connor. "Really? Can't you come up with a better line?"

"Answer your cell phone."

It was sitting in the office. "I'm at work. You really need a room?"

"Moki wants to go to the lake. You game?"

The other phone rang, and Jaya answered it. "Crescent hotel . . ."

"Ty?"

"I'll call you later. Some of us have work to do." An unfair jab, since Connor was stuck running his mom's store.

"Fine. Fix that hotel."

Tyson hung up, grumbling to himself. Fix the hotel. Right.

Time to see what Miss scaredy-pants on the fourth floor needed.

Turned out she didn't need anything. Instead of reassuring her that the ghost didn't haunt the fourth floor, Tyson discovered she'd taken a series of photographs that she believed showed a portrait of Michael. Tyson spent an hour humoring her, telling her to submit the photographs to the hotel for analyzation.

Crazy patrons.

He stepped into the office, welcoming the short reprieve from people. He spent half an hour going over the books to make sure everything was in proper order. He woke the computer up and set his laptop beside it. He should have some free time today, and it was law-school application season.

Again.

He jammed his finger into the top of the desk, a knot of anxiety rolling around in his chest. He'd taken the LSAT three years ago, right before he graduated with his bachelor's. But every time he started to fill out applications, something held him back.

Fear of failure.

He pulled out the sandwich he'd bought from the restaurant and once again pulled up the list of schools he'd made. He checked websites, made sure the schools were still ones he was interested in, updated their application fees, and jotted down the dates they were accepting applications.

And that was as far as he got. He tapped his hand on his yellow legal pad, feeling no closer to becoming a lawyer than three years ago. And the longer he was out of school, the less confident he felt that he ever would be one.

Which would only prove his mom right.

He dug his fingers through his hair, pulling at the wavy locks.

A knock came on the office door, and Tyson welcomed the distraction. "Yeah."

The door opened, and Jaya poked her head inside. "Linda is on the phone, she wants to talk to you."

"Who is Linda?" They had a Linda on the payroll? Tyson thought he knew all the employees.

Jaya lifted a shoulder. "I guess she does some of the tours tonight."

"Oh." Tyson followed Jaya out of the office. He couldn't be expected to remember all of the ghost tour people. They had several tours each evening, and it wasn't always the same tour guide. He picked up the phone, pulling up the reservation screen on the computer at the same time. She probably just wanted to know how many people were in her groups that night.

"This is Tyson. How can I help you?"

"Mr. Hafford?"

He straightened up. "Yes, ma'am."

She cleared her throat. "I've got three tours I'm supposed to give tonight, the six o'clock, seven-thirty, and the nine o'clock." Her voice came out scratchy and thick. "But I'm super sick. Can you find someone to take my groups for me?"

Nuh-uh. This was well outside his domain. "I'm sorry you don't feel well, ma'am. But isn't that your responsibility?" Tyson did his best to sound polite and respectful rather than reveal the extent of his annoyance. He would not add "find substitute tour-guides" to his job description.

"I can't find the list of subs," she said, her voice weaker than before. "And I can barely keep my eyes open to look. I don't think I could call anyone even if I found it."

Oh brother. Tyson rolled his eyes.

"If we don't find someone," she went on, "you'll have to cancel the tours. Hopefully they can reschedule. But if they can't, they might leave negative reviews. People are weird that way."

"What about combining one of your tours with a different group?"

"Sure, if the other groups aren't sold out. You can check."

Back to him again. He ground his teeth together, seeing no way out of this. "You don't worry about a thing, Miss Linda. I will get it all taken care of. You just rest up and get better."

"Thank you, Mr. Hafford. I knew I could count on you."

More like take advantage of him. Tyson kept a smile on his

face until he hung up, then he rolled his eyes at Kevin and Jaya. "Brother. Now I have to find someone else to take her ghost tours."

"Don't look at me," Kevin said.

"I wasn't looking at either of you." Tyson opened the filing cabinet and searched for the file with the contracted employees. "Both of you would be horrible tour guides."

"Thanks for the vote of confidence," Kevin said.

"Hey, I'm all about the cop out." Jaya lifted her hands in the air. "I do what I'm told and punch the time clock. Don't ask me to be funny."

Tyson spent the next hour figuring out replacements for the three tours. The six o'clock tour he mingled with the six-thirty tour, since both only had a few people, and all of the guests were agreeable. And he only had to call four names on the list of subs before he found someone willing to cover the seven-thirty tour.

But he couldn't get anyone for the nine o'clock.

He called every name on the list of subs and left a message for every person he didn't speak to.

No one was available.

At five o'clock he did the rounds in the hotel, making sure the restaurant was ready for the evening and the bathrooms cleaned. He checked that the front desk was well-stocked and then sat down in the office, wasting time. He should go home, but not having a replacement for the ghost tour nagged at him.

"What time are you off, Jaya?" Tyson asked as he came back to the check-in desk, even though he knew her schedule.

"I'm off at eight." She eyed him. "You're not considering me for the ghost tour, are you?"

"I'm getting a little desperate," Tyson admitted. "I've left messages with all the substitutes. If I don't find someone, I'll have to cancel the tour. And even with full refunds, people are never happy with that."

Jaya shrugged. "Then cancel it. There are worse things than a few negative reviews. And they won't affect our sales."

No, no, they wouldn't, but Mr. Draper hated it when anyone was unhappy with the hotel, and Tyson took his job too personally not to care.

"Hey, quit fretting so much." Jaya's face was stern, but one corner of her mouth lifted up. She shrugged. "I'm sure it's going to be fine. It's not like someone died. If any of the subs call here, I'll give them your number."

"I gave them my number." Tyson eyed her and sighed. He should have known Jays would be too cynical to think a silly thing like a canceled ghost tour was a big deal. "If any of them call here instead of me, they're trying to avoid me." He stashed his name badge into a drawer and grabbed his car keys. "I guess we'll just hope for the best."

Tyson made the ten-minute drive out to Van Buren highway and pulled his car into the driveway of the house he'd grown up in. The car clock showed it was only six-fifteen. He still had two more hours to find a sub before the unthinkable happened.

He pushed open the door of his car and walked up the drive, spotting the hammock he and his younger brother had stretched between two twisted trees when they were younger. There wasn't much of a backyard, the hillside was too steep; but they'd made good use of the front.

It was just Tyson now. Nobody else lived here. His parents made him pay rent, but it mostly just covered the utilities. He thought he should feel grateful, but he saw the way his mom sneered every time she told someone he still lived at home. Like he wasn't capable of doing anything on his own. But moving out to find a small apartment felt like cutting his nose off to spite his face, so . . .

He threw his keys on the counter and wandered into the kitchen for a drink. The clock on the stove glared at him. 6:20. He opened the freezer and pulled out a burrito, then nuked it, all while obsessively checking his phone. His people were lame. Didn't any of them want to make extra money today? Maybe Connor would do it. No, he was too serious to be a ghost guide. Moki could.

Even as he considered it, Tyson dismissed the thought. Moki had never even been on the ghost tour, while Tyson had made himself sit through it several times just for this particular scenario.

He downed the rest of his Coke, then crumpled the can in his hands. He was going to need a stronger drink.

AMBER

J ust as Amber suspected, by the time she got Raven home, she seemed perfectly normal again. Amber fought back the frustration and settled down to get as much work done as she could.

Her phone rang right as Amber was getting Raven up from her nap, and she took a moment to check the caller ID before answering. If it was Violet, she would have to step into the other room.

She smiled when she saw the word "Mom" dancing across the screen. She answered with one swipe, speaking softly so as not to wake Raven. "Hey, Mom. Are you close?"

"We'll be there in ten minutes," her mom, Ruth, said. "Would you like us to meet you somewhere or go to your apartment?"

"Oh, I'm at home. So you may as well just come here."

"Why are you at home? I thought you'd be working."

"I am." Amber sighed. "Raven got sick and I had to pick her up from daycare. So I'm working from here."

Raven opened her eyes as Amber spoke and reached her

arms out toward her. "Mommy."

"I hear her now," her mom said, warmth in her voice. "What is she sick with?"

"I don't think she is." Amber gathered Raven in her arms and carried her into the living room, propping the phone up with her shoulder. "She's been getting these fevers just long enough for the day care to call home. Usually by the time she wakes up from a nap, she's fine."

"Well, that's odd," Ruth said. "Have you taken her to the doctor?"

"No. Should I? I keep thinking there's nothing wrong."

"It might not hurt to get her looked at."

"Yeah, I suppose." More time she'd have to take off work. But what if something were wrong with Raven? She would hate herself if she didn't take her to the doctor. She secured Raven in the booster seat and gave her a sippy cup and a handful of goldfish crackers.

"Feel free to take advantage of me while I'm here. I don't mind watching Raven."

"Yeah, I know." But Amber's stomach tightened in disagreement with the idea. She'd only managed to graduate college because her parents took care of Raven. That wasn't their job. Raven was Amber's daughter, Amber's responsibility. She was determined not to use other people to pay for her mistakes.

Not a mistake, she amended as Raven tossed her sippy cup at the wall and splattered juice on the cabinets. An accident. An unexpected consequence. But definitely not a mistake.

Her parents pulled into the apartment complex three minutes later, and Raven lit up at the sight of them, chattering excitedly with every vocal sound she knew how to make.

"Oh, you're getting so big!" Ruth said, plucking Raven out

of the booster seat and spinning her around. Raven laughed. Ruth beamed. "She looks just like you when you were little."

"Mom. We know that's not true." Raven had too much of her father in her, with the ebony black hair and dark, dark eyes. Most days Amber did not even attempt to tame the wild curls flying around Raven's face.

"You don't see it. But these cheeks, the way she crinkles her nose and smiles. Just like you."

"Well, she is mine." A warm pride replaced some of the tightness in her chest.

Amber's dad Bruce was waiting his turn to snuggle Raven, and Ruth handed the little girl over. Her mom put a hand on Amber's arm and guided her into the living room.

"So, what do you think about the new body parts they dug up?"

Amber knew immediately to what her mother referred, and she shuddered. It was all over the news, how the gardeners at the Crescent Hotel had dug up jars of Norman Baker's fermented body parts. The crazy fake doctor had done experiments on people staying at his cancer hospital in the early 1900s. Thanks to him and a number of other random deaths, the Crescent Hotel was considered the most haunted hotel in America.

"Creepy." Why people would choose the hotel as a wedding location was beyond Amber. But they did, and it was her job to accommodate.

"So." A devilish glint entered her mother's eyes. "I've heard they incorporated the body parts into the ghost tour. I've got tickets for the nine o'clock tour."

"Nine?" Now was her chance to talk her mom out of this. "That's so late. I have to get home to put Raven to bed."

Her mom tsked. "You think your dad's not capable? He's

done the bedtime thing before."

It was no use. Amber tried one last-ditch plea. "It's a waste of fifty bucks. You know I don't take any of that stuff seriously."

"On the contrary. I know this stuff freaks you out." Ruth wiggled her eyebrows up-and-down. "Come on. Humor me. I've already got the tickets."

Amber shook her head. Her mom had a fascination for all things supernatural and macabre, while Amber's thoughts tended to go in the complete opposite direction, preferring pink fluffy unicorns and sappy love stories. She tried to say that she didn't believe in ghosts, but the truth was she hoped her disbelief could make them not real.

"Fine. But only because you've got tickets. And Dad, you're okay watching Raven?"

She need not have asked. The two of them had crawled inside Raven's pop-up castle-tent, and the little girl squealed every time her grandpa nudged her with his face and brayed like a donkey.

"Great, that's settled," Ruth said, checking her watch. "If we leave now, we can catch dinner before the tour, maybe even do some shopping on the strip."

Amber grabbed her purse. She stepped over to Raven and gave her a big hug. "Be good for Grandpa, will you?"

Raven nodded and squirmed away from her mother.

Amber cast a glance over her shoulder as she stepped out the door. Her mother put a hand on her forearm and squeezed.

"She'll be fine, sweetie."

"I know," Amber admitted. She climbed into the passenger seat beside her mother. "I just hate to leave her. Especially with this fever she's been getting. What if she gets sick while

Dad is watching her?"

"If you're worried, why don't you take her to the doctor? It's worth the time off to get the peace of mind."

"All right, I will. If she spikes a fever again, I'll make an appointment." Saying the resolution aloud brought a sense of relief to Amber's mind. She had a plan of action now.

They moseyed along the strip for an hour before enjoying a pleasant dinner at the Rogue's Manor. But as they pulled away in the car and headed the mile up the curvy road to the Crescent Hotel, Amber had second thoughts.

"This place is creepy at night, Mom."

"The sun is only just now going down and there's plenty of light. Besides, you're familiar with this hotel. How many weddings do you do here a month?"

"At least three," Amber said. "This wasn't a happy place. Even when it was a girls' college, lots of bad things happened."

"And lots of good things too, I'm sure." Ruth parked the car and got out, and Amber reluctantly followed. Sure, lots of good things had probably happened here, but the happy spirits didn't linger to haunt the guests.

Ruth hooked an arm through Amber's as they walked past the fountain out front with the sculpture of a crescent moon. "I haven't heard you mention any boys."

Amber pulled her arm away with a flash of irritation. "I'm not dating." And she didn't want to be.

"Well, maybe it's better that way."

"Why?" Amber said, her hackles up. "Because I'm not smart enough to find the right kind of guy?"

"No, of course not, sweetie. But last time you dated, there was that fiasco with Raven . . ."

"I won't make that mistake again," Amber said. "Nobody

meets Raven unless we've been dating at least a month."

"And there was the guy before that who only wanted—"

"He made assumptions about me because I have a kid, and I was stupid enough not to realize it," Amber interrupted. "Believe me, I'll be keeping things on the down-low next time."

"And of course there was Drake—"

"Mom!" Amber stopped walking and glared at her mom. "I get it. I'm a failure when it comes to dating. So I'm not dating." But suddenly, she wanted to be. She wanted to be the girl in the romance story who found the perfect guy, the one who loved all of her and gave all of himself. A deep longing filled her heart. Why couldn't she have that?

"You're not a failure, you just—"

"Mom. Let's just do this ghost tour."

Her mother exhaled. "Yes. I'm sorry. I don't want to see you hurt again."

"One more word, and I'm walking home."

Ruth pressed her lips together and kept quiet. Amber followed her into the hotel and fell behind her as she went up to the ticket desk, lost in her own thoughts.

Only one person was working the front desk, and he was helping a customer with the self-serve kiosk on the corner.

"If you want to go on tonight's tour, just pick this date and then choose the number of tickets. Yes, like that."

The door to the banquet room opened and closed at the end of the hallway, and a young man dressed smartly in a button up shirt with pressed trousers came down the hall, staring at a clipboard. He lifted his eyes as he approached the desk, a distracted smile on his face as he scanned the waiting clientele. His gaze landed on Amber, and his smile brightened.

"Hi," he said, opening a waist-high door to step behind the

counter. "Can I help you?"

He seemed vaguely familiar, but Amber couldn't place him.

"Yes, we have will-call tickets for the nine o'clock tour," her mother said, showing a digital receipt.

"Fantastic. Just take the hallway behind you and go up the four flights of stairs—you know what, I'm headed that way. I'll take you there."

"Oh. That's nice of you."

"Did you want to take the stairs or the elevator?" he asked as they passed a white-brick fireplace and the lounge with an antique organ.

"We can take the stairs. We are young and fit," Ruth said with a wide smile.

He laughed, setting a quick pace as they crossed the hall to the staircase, a winding angular structure with an open railing. More than a hundred years old, the stairs leaned slightly, inclining toward the stairwell. Amber stayed well away from the center. She never had a reason to climb the stairs during weddings, and she avoided looking over the edge as they wound upward four flights. The middle remained open, and she knew a glance down the interior would give her a dizzying vertigo.

The man turned at the top of the fourth floor and gestured toward a room. "Go inside and find a seat. Your tour guide will be here in just a moment. If you need anything—" He reached into his pocket and pulled out a business card. "I'm the hotel manager; you can just let me know. Enjoy your tour." His eyes met Amber's, and he gave a sheepish grin before nodding at her mother and continuing down the hall.

Amber looked at the card in her hand, wondering why the hotel manager thought they might need him. Tyson Hafford. It had a nice ring to it.

"Well, I'll say he went above and beyond," her mom said. "I guess he's hoping for a good review."

"I'm sure you're right." Amber tucked the business card into her purse and sat with her mom in the back row of folding chairs set up in the room. Old-fashioned portraits and ancient newspaper articles hung in frames on the walls. She tried not to pay close attention to any of them. Somehow it creeped her out even more to think of them as real people instead of the faceless dead.

A few other guests joined them, standing around the room before plopping themselves into chairs.

The tour guide was easy to spot when he came in, dressed in a 1900-style suit, a top-hat, and a mustache. "Welcome, welcome to our ghost tour this evening."

His voice came out crisp and dry, like an old piece of paper. His eyes flicked to hers and a hue crept up his cheeks before he faced the crowd. "Let me tell you a bit about—"

Amber gasped quietly. "Mom! It's the hotel manager!"

"It can't be." Ruth leaned forward and narrowed her eyes, and Amber was certain she was right. He'd changed clothes and stuck on a mustache, and he was studiously avoiding her eyes.

"It is!" Amber giggled, suddenly enjoying the tour a lot more.

Tyson Hafford moved the group into the hallway and explained the history behind the beautiful paintings.

"I encourage you to take lots of pictures," he said. "You never know what might show up."

"Pass," Amber muttered. If there were ghosts around, she'd rather not know.

Excited guests snapped photos like crazy. Amber glanced at the sky room café as they passed and snatched at her mom.

"Sure you don't just want to go sit down and grab some more dessert?"

"And miss seeing the jars of body parts that the crazy doctor collected?" She gave Amber a disapproving look.

"Right," Amber murmured.

"And over here at this railing," Tyson was saying, "a maid lost track of her child for a moment. These non-safety-regulated rails are just the right size for a toddler to slip through."

Amber pressed a hand to her mouth. She peeked over the side and shuddered, imagining the horrible scene. She could just picture the frantic mother searching for her child, realizing with each passing moment what must have happened . . .

A hand touched her shoulder, and she looked up to see his gaze on her.

"Careful," he said, removing his hand. "Don't get too close to the edge."

He stepped away from her, but Amber's eyes followed him as he merged back into the crowd.

TYSON

Why, oh why, was she on this tour?

Tyson fumbled over his presentation as he led the group to the second floor. He hoped he wasn't mixing up the words as he pointed out the wonky architecture, because all he could think about was the cute brunette and her mother, who kept looking at him and laughing.

Most mortifying night ever.

He stopped by Michael's room. "This room books up a year in advance with single young women eager to meet the handsome and charismatic Michael."

The mother chuckled. "There you go, Amber. You're single. A dead boyfriend is a safe one."

"Ha ha." Amber's face grew red, and she shot a glance at Tyson. He pretended not to notice.

So she didn't have a boyfriend. Good to know.

The tour continued back down to the first floor. Tyson stopped in the lobby, his eyes darting around as he searched for the woman who had said she could relieve him. They'd made an agreement . . . She'd promised to take over the last half of the tour for him.

"And that impression in the chair is from Morris the cat. He's dead. So don't sit on him."

There she was. She came in with a purple wig and a string of pearls, and she waved excitedly. Tyson exhaled. Why couldn't she have shown up earlier?

"As you begin your descent to the morgue, folks, I'm going to turn you over to my trustworthy colleague. It's been a pleasure." He bowed to a smattering of applause from the group, and he couldn't help glancing at Amber.

Her eyes flicked out the double glass doors leading outside to the morgue, and if he wasn't mistaken, she looked petrified.

Tyson stepped back to the counter while the tour guide took over. She continued the dialog, and he stuffed the mustache into his top hat, then stuck both under the counter. Ian was working the reception desk, and he didn't even glance at Tyson.

The group moved out the door. Except Amber, who stood frozen. Then she turned around, looking ready to dart into the parking lot.

Tyson cleared his throat, attracting her attention. "Your tour going okay?"

Her eyes went wide as if surprised to see him there. A little smile lifted her lips, and she said, "I'm not much of a ghost groupie."

The group was gone now, hustled outside by the tour guide.

"I've never actually seen a ghost here, if it helps," Tyson said. He lifted one shoulder. "Bit of a bummer. It's why I got a job here."

She moved toward the counter, her smile broader now. "That would be a let down."

"Seriously." Tyson nodded. "If I don't see one soon, I'm getting a job at a different haunted hotel."

She put her arms on the counter and rested her chin on them. "I don't think anyone will notice if I skip the morgue."

"You don't want to see the new body parts they found?" Tyson also rested his hands on the counter, leaning toward her. "It's fascinating. We're still trying to figure out what half of them are."

"No thanks."

"You can stay here if you want. The group will come back after the morgue tour."

"Thank you. I think I will." Her eyes wandered over his face, studying him. "It's Tyson, right?"

She knew his name. She'd read his business card. Why did that make him feel like singing?

"Yeah. And you're Amber?"

She gave him a startled look. "How did you know that?"

Well, if he hadn't known already, her mom would have given it away. "We met a few days ago. When you did a wedding here."

"Oh!" She gasped, pushing away from the counter as a rosy hue crept up her cheeks. "I thought I knew you somehow!"

"Hotel managers are real memorable," he teased.

She pressed a hand to her forehead. "I feel like an idiot."

"Don't worry, I'm sure you'll remember me now."

She groaned again, and he laughed. He liked her more than ever.

"Can I get you something to drink?"

She tilted her head. "What have you got?"

He shrugged. "The bar is open upstairs. Pretty much anything you want I can get."

She considered him, tucking a piece of hair behind her ear. "I'll take a glass of water."

"That's it? I can do better than that."

She tilted her face upward, and her mouth seemed particularly flirtatious. "Surprise me."

Oh, how he wanted to. Wouldn't she be surprised if he kissed her now? *Get a grip, Tyson,* he chided himself, mentally slapping his face. "One surprise coming right up."

He slipped away from the counter and went to the kitchen of the Crystal Dining Room restaurant, but not before he saw the smile on her face. It warmed him inside, and he put his bartending skills to work behind the bar, making a simple mocktail of club soda, lemonade, and strawberries. He didn't dare presume to make something stronger. She might get all kinds of wrong ideas about his intentions.

Or maybe they wouldn't be so wrong.

When he returned, Amber had seated herself on the sofa next to the automated piano and was looking through the ghost photo book on the coffee table. Tyson handed her the drink and settled down beside her.

"Fascinating photos, right?"

"They are interesting," Amber agreed. "Do you get new ones often?"

"Oh, all the time. Just this morning there was this little old lady who swore to me she had a million photographs of Michael."

"Michael." Amber lifted her head and focused on the door across from them, nodding. "The super flirtatious ghost."

"That would be him. Michael the womanizer."

"And was he womanizing this patron?"

"If he was, his tastes have definitely matured with time."

It took Amber a moment to get the context behind his words, and then she laughed. "Maybe he has matured as well." She took a sip of her drink and stood up. "I think I'm feeling brave enough to join everyone in the morgue now."

He nodded and stood also. "Hey." He lifted his eyebrows like it was a spontaneous thought, not something he'd been considering for the past half hour. His heart pounded a little harder. "Maybe we could hang sometime when I'm not on the clock. What's your number?" *Smooth*, he congratulated himself.

"Yeah, maybe. I've got your number. I'll reach out."

Slam. The whole, "Don't call us, we'll call you." "Sounds good." He moved behind the check-in desk and perused the guest list, keeping his eyes down as she walked outside. No biggie. Wasn't like it was the first time he'd been rejected.

Beside him, Ian cleared his throat. "Well. That was certainly interesting."

Tyson rolled his eyes at his employee, five years older than him with ambitions to be a professional video gamer. "What, watching me get shot down?"

"Watching you try to flirt."

"I know how to flirt," Tyson said, miffed.

"You're definitely out of practice. My mom could've done better than that."

"Well, maybe she and I should hook up," Tyson grumbled, which only made Ian laugh.

The lights in the main room flickered, and then they went out.

"And we just lost power," Ian said.

Obvious. But Tyson's thoughts were already racing to a certain tour group in the morgue with a certain girl who wasn't a huge fan of ghosts to begin with. He pulled open the drawer, his hands closing on one of several magnum flashlights they kept there. "I'll be right back."

"You checking on the breaker?"

He should. That was usually the cause of electrical problems in this old building. "Yep. You call the electrical company, see if there are any outages." Probably not. It wasn't that unusual for this to happen.

"Did the power just go out?" a man's voice shouted from down the hallways.

Tyson lifted his flashlight and shown it that direction, and Mr. Draper shielded his eyes from the bright beam, his salt and pepper build reflecting the white light. Tyson shot a glare at Ian.

"You didn't tell me Mr. Draper was here," he hissed.

"I forgot. He just stepped in for a moment to check on one of the rooms."

"Sorry, Mr. Draper," Tyson called. "It's not a big deal. I'll find out what caused it."

Tyson hurried outside, the powerful beam of the flashlight shining on his path, more anxious about the young lady in the morgue than the breaker. But the breaker was closer, so he stopped and did a quick check. All in working order. It was an actual power outage this time.

He made a beeline for the morgue steps. He imagined a group of panicked tourists, clutching each other in the dark morgue or fumbling against the walls, afraid to touch anything but trying to find the way out.

He rounded the corner and drew up short. Amber leaned against the brick exterior, face illuminated by the screen of her phone, her eyes down as her thumb scrolled. He approached slowly.

"Is everything okay?" he asked.

She looked up, then straightened, a flicker of surprise showing in her eyes. Great. Now he looked like a stalker.

"Everything's fine. Why?"

"Well. The power went out in the hotel. So." He brandished his flashlight. "I came to make sure the tour was okay."

"Oh. I didn't know."

So much for being a knight in shining armor. "I'll just see how everyone is."

He pushed the door open and heard the laughter inside. The tour guide turned around and flashed him a smile. A dozen tiny lights flickered in the dark room.

Right. Everyone with a phone had a flashlight in their pocket.

"We lost power," he stated lamely. "Everyone good?"

"Best tour ever," a woman giggled. "That sure frightened me!"

They echoed her sentiment.

"Great. Glad it all worked out." Tyson backed out and found Amber watching him. He nodded at her on his way to the sidewalk, trying to hold his head up during his walk of shame.

He heaved a sigh. Time to call it a night.

Chapter Four

AMBER

"So, tell me about that guy," Amber's mom needled as she maneuvered the car through the narrow switchback streets of Eureka Springs.

Amber lifted a shoulder and chewed on her lower lip for a moment before answering. "There's really not much to tell. I just met him a few days ago."

"And yet you had a drink with him?" Her mother's eyebrows lifted delicately.

A short laugh escaped Amber's lips, and she remembered the flustered expression on Tyson's face when he found her outside the morgue. "I felt bad for him."

"So you sat with him out of pity?" Ruth gave her a sideways look. "That's not the best way to start things off."

"Yeah . . ." It was cute that he had run to her rescue even if it hadn't been needed. And the way his cheeks had flushed only reinforced the image of a boy trying to fit into a man's shoes. "What do you care what the motive is?"

"Honey, anyone you date needs to be able to take care of you and Raven."

The words rankled Amber all wrong. "I'm not looking for anyone to take care of me. We've got this on our own."

Her mother held up an apologetic hand. "Okay. Sorry. Wrong words. I know you're very capable."

Amber let out a breath and forced herself to relax. "Sorry," she mumbled. It was a touchy subject for her. But if she chose to become involved with a guy, it would be because he enhanced her life and made her happy, not because she needed him to survive.

Raven was long asleep by the time Amber and her mom walked in the door. Her dad sat watching the Food Network on TV, which made Amber giggle. He was such a foodie.

"You know, we have some interesting cooks right here in Eureka Springs," Amber said, hopping onto the couch next to him. "There's a local guy that has a MeTube channel. You should check him out."

"Oh yeah?" Her dad looked interested. "What's his name?"

"I'm not sure, Mic something or other. Sometimes he's a guest chef at restaurants in the area. We could track him down if you want."

"So you and your boyfriend can go on a date there?" her mom teased.

"Boyfriend? You're dating someone?" Her dad looked worried.

Amber sighed in irritation. "No," she said, more sharply than she intended. "How was everything with Raven? Did she spike a fever?"

"No fever, no problem at all. She was a breeze. I put her to bed about two hours ago."

Not surprising, but it relieved her to know Raven hadn't acted sick. "Thanks, Dad. You guys are staying here, right?"

"We don't want to infringe on you—" her dad said, just as

her mom said, "We're planning on it."

Her parents looked at each other, and Amber laughed. "I was planning on it also. I put an air mattress in Raven's room. I'll sleep there, you guys can have my room."

She saw her dad start to protest, but her mother swatted his arm. "Bruce. You know we both don't fit on that air mattress. Just say thank you and be grateful our daughter is so thoughtful."

"I still want to know about this guy you're dating," her dad said, apparently accepting his fate.

"I'm not," Amber said. "There's just a boy I met at the hotel. He hasn't asked me out, so don't plan a wedding yet."

Did she imagine it, or did her father looked relieved?

"Well, I know you won't rush into anything," her dad began. "Just remember—"

"Spare me the lecture," Amber interrupted. "I heard it all from Mom in the car. And believe me, I know about the birds and the bees and how it all works." She pushed past her parents and went down the hall to Raven's room, but the murmur of their voices carried down the hall.

"Seems a bit touchy," Bruce said.

"We have a habit of pushing her buttons," her mom said. "She's an adult, and we need to give her space. She's not the same little girl from a few years ago."

Amber gently closed her door so they wouldn't hear it and know she'd been listening. Maybe she was defensive. But it was true. The naïve, blissfully-in-love twenty-year-old girl who had gotten pregnant three years earlier no longer existed. Time and experience had jaded her worldview.

Raven made a soft, sleepy noise in her toddler bed, and Amber tiptoed over to see her. She ran a hand over Raven's black curls, and her heart softened with such an intense swelling of affection that it brought tears to Amber's eyes.

Romance was no fairytale, and motherhood was no walk in the park. But she and Raven, together as a family, were the greatest reality Amber could hope for.

TYSON

The boat rocked as someone else climbed aboard, but Tyson didn't open his eyes. The sunglasses shielded him from the sun's incessant rays. Even though it was barely past nine in the morning, already he felt the prickly warning of sunburn on his skin.

Someone jostled his leg, and a cold liquid dripped on his stomach.

"Moki," Tyson said, sitting up and grabbing a towel. He knew without looking it would be his less-than-graceful friend.

"Sorry," Moki said, grinning at him as he settled on a boat cushion across from Tyson, drink in hand.

He wouldn't burn, not with that dark skin. "Nice beadwork," Tyson said, mocking the colorful balls Moki had added to his meticulous dreads. That had to be an oxymoron. Weren't dreads supposed to be the epitome of hair not taken care of?

"Thanks." Moki's smile didn't flinch. "Aren't you a ray of sunshine?"

"We've got plenty of that." Tyson fished a bottle of sunscreen from the side of the boat and lathered up.

"He's been the life of the party since he arrived," Connor said. He stood behind the wheel and maneuvered the boat away from the dock. "Got a bee in his pants or something."

Tyson ignored his friends and opened the cooler, retrieving a drink. The can popped open with a satisfying hiss, and Tyson looked out across the shimmering water of Beaver Lake as he sipped.

"Hey." Moki leaned over and slapped his knee. "There's another hotel opening on the highway. Bet they'd hire you."

He and Connor both laughed like it was hilarious, but Tyson didn't break a smile. "I'm not leaving the Crescent until I see a ghost."

"Good luck, then," Connor said.

"Let me know when it happens," Moki added.

Connor waved to another boater and pulled to a halt near a cove. "We getting out and swimming? Or pulling out the tubes?"

"We gotta tube while we still have this boat," Moki said. "When Dave and your mom break up, he'll take this with him, and bye-bye lake days."

"I'll drive," Tyson said, pushing to his feet. "You guys can tube."

"I don't mind driving," Connor said, his eyes on Tyson. "You can tube."

"Looks like I'm first." Moki set to work attaching the flotation device to the rope and throwing it overboard.

"You okay?" Connor asked, his voice lowered.

Tyson glanced back at Moki as the big guy shrugged into a life jacket just a tad bit too small. "Oh, it's nothing. I'm a little down."

"Why?"

Tyson hesitated. It was silly, wasn't it, to feel this way?

There was a splash as Moki jumped into the water, and a moment later he sprawled across the intertube. "I'm ready!"

Connor threw another glance at Tyson but just yelled, "Hang on tight!" He put the boat into gear and circled away, and the engine noise prevented them from further conversation. Moki yelled and whooped like a seventh-grade girl.

"Knock him off!" Tyson shouted.

"I'm trying!" Connor made a sharp turn, and the boat rocked as it plowed over the wakes it had just made. Moki's tube followed, bouncing and jostling with each one. Moki clung to the handles, cheering.

"You failed."

"I'll get him."

Tyson couldn't help grinning. He'd met Connor six years earlier during their freshman year of college. Connor had ended up dropping out to take care of his grandma's-slash-mom's store, but they'd stayed friends. Connor tended to be the serious one in their trio, while Moki gladly played the part of the clown.

Tyson just hoped he fit in.

It took two more tries, but Connor did succeed in knocking Moki off the tube.

"You can go next," Tyson said as Connor drove the boat back to Moki.

"I'll let Moki have some fun for a bit. He's nothing but an overgrown kid anyway."

"No kidding," Tyson snorted.

"So what's with you?"

Tyson looked down at his can and fiddled with the tab. "It's nothing."

"Yeah, right."

"No, really. It's nothing."

"It's a girl."

Tyson squinted at his friend. "How did you know?"

"Because not even talking about law school gets you this flustered."

Tyson had to smile. "Yeah. It's a girl."

"Well, who is it? Do I get to meet her?"

"She won't even give me her phone number."

Connor laughed. His dark eyes were hidden behind the sunglasses, but Tyson could imagine how they teased him. "Want me to get it for you?"

"Shut up," he growled.

"Ready!" Moki shouted.

They fell silent while the motor roared. Moki finally fell off again, and the motor quieted as Connor turned around to pick him up.

"When will you see her again?" he asked.

"I don't know. Sometimes I see her at work. I gave her my number, but I don't think she'll call."

"So you've at least talked to her."

"Yes." Tyson glared.

"What's her name?"

"Amber. Amber Morris."

Connor shrugged. "Small town. I'll keep an eye out."

"I don't need your help."

"Yes, you do."

Tyson played with his friends at the lake until after lunch, and then Connor had to head to the strip and work his mom's store. It was a good opportunity for Tyson to get his law school applications done, anyway.

He pulled up the list and stared at it. Then he reorganized it. Then he opened up five different schools in five different windows on the computer and studied them. He read their requirements again, what they expected of their students. What GPA he would need to maintain.

His stomach knotted. His mom always said he wasn't the smart one. She said he wouldn't amount to much. When he majored in philosophy, thinking it would be a good precursor to law school, she said she'd always known he would pick a useless career.

He'd planned to show her. He'd taken the LSAT his senior year, ready to apply to schools and prove to his mom that he could do something.

And then he'd gotten scared.

Here he was two years later, too afraid of failure to even take that first step.

"You're an excellent hotel manager," his mom had told him when he saw his parents at Christmas. She'd said it with satisfaction in her eyes. Certain she'd made the correct judgment about her second son.

He could do this. He wanted to be a lawyer. He wanted to follow in his dad's steps, just like his older brother had. But Michael could do no wrong. Even when he was suspended for illegal drug use his sophomore year, all he got was a slap on the hand. And when he lost his scholarship the first year of law school, his parents took out a second mortgage to help him pay his tuition.

Do this, Tyson told himself. He forced himself to find the essay questions from each school and write them down. He could at least keep the topics in the back of his mind, and maybe some would overlap so he could use the same essay for multiple schools.

He looked again at his list and the application due dates. Some started taking applications in September, others not until November.

He had six weeks to get his head in the right spot.

This would be his year. He would do it. He couldn't sit here in mediocrity any longer.

Chapter Five

AMBER

"These aren't the kinds of flowers I want." Erica, the bride-to-be, scrunched up her nose as she flipped through the photos Mr. Connor had sent over. "I want them more like the big bright colored flowers you see in Hawaii. As if it were a tropical wedding." She tapped the paper with the tip of a manicured fingernail. "I wrote that down already."

"Well, yes, I know," Amber said, trying to hold onto her patience. She hoped this bride wouldn't turn into a Bridezilla. She hated working with those. "But you're not on Hawaii, so those flowers don't grow naturally here."

"But you can get them, right?" Erica lowered her chin and arched her penciled eyebrows, her expression rather intimidating. "Just for a few hours."

"You're absolutely right," Amber said. "The wedding is only for a few hours. But we will prep the venue the night before, and we'll get the flowers in that morning. If they're shipping from somewhere far away, we need to have them arrive the day of the event to preserve them. The florist will have to do special shipping and delivery, and it will be a lot more expensive."

"How much more are we talking?" Erica asked, tilting her head to the side.

"I can get you an official estimate in a few hours. I need to check my sources and see what kind of deal we can work."

Erica nodded. "Okay. That sounds reasonable." She straightened up, shouldering her purse. "You'll call me?"

Amber stood as well. "As soon as I have the information, I'll contact you."

"Thank you. Thank you for showing me my options."

Amber walked her out of the office, then let out a careful breath. Clients hated hearing budgeting issues, but that hadn't gone too badly.

The office phone rang as Amber typed up an email to Mr. Connor outlining the bride's needs and desires. Probably another client. She let it ring, knowing they'd leave a message, and she could call them back at her leisure.

She pulled up the last email Mr. Connor had sent her, with sample photos and Lilly's ideas for how to transform an Arkansas wedding to look exotic. It might be possible. But having various pricing options would be valuable.

The phone dinged, indicating the caller had left message.

Amber sent the email. She grabbed notepad and pen and pressed the Playback button on the office phone.

"Hi, this is Tyson Hafford, manager of the Crescent Hotel."

His voice carried over the line, carrying a note of boyishness that tugged at her heart. Amber nearly dropped the pen in surprise.

"If you could please have Amber Morris call me back at this number, I would really appreciate it. Thank you."

The message ended after he gave his number, and a flurry of

conflicting emotions chased each other through Amber's chest. Pleasure that he had tracked her down through work and actually called, excitement that he was interested, anxiety about returning the call, and fear for the future. Too many emotions to analyze at once.

She turned back to her computer and told herself to worry about it later.

❧

Mr. Connor called about forty minutes later. "I just got your email. Can you meet me over at the house? I've got some ideas."

"Sure. I'll be there soon."

The screen door opened before Amber even made it up the walk, and Mr. Connor stepped out.

"Come around back, I want to show you what I was thinking."

Amber followed him around to the back of the house where a trellis garden rose several feet out of the ground. Mr. Connor put his hands behind a pink bloom as large as his palm.

"It's a hibiscus plant!" Amber cried in surprise.

"A rose mallow, to be exact," Mr. Connor said, a pleased expression on his face. "It's a hardier variety than the Hawaiian version and doesn't get as tall. But these flourish all over the garden. We do have this smaller hibiscus and jasmine growing right here on the grounds. Using what I've got can help bring down her overall cost. I talked to Lilly, and she suggested we outsource to a nursery for a few birds of paradise and plumeria blooms as accent flowers."

Excitement stirred in Amber's chest, and she nodded eagerly. "This is great." Always a bonus when they could deliver what the bride wanted for less than expected.

Mr. Connor nodded. "Then I'll include an estimate that has

these instead of the imported plants. She can compare them and decide what she wants to do."

An engine revved, and the sound of tires kicking up gravel came from around the front of the house.

Mr. Connor cocked his head. "I wonder who's here? We don't get a lot of company out here." He moved back around to the front of the house, and Amber followed because she didn't know what else to do.

A green sedan sat in the driveway, and a man with broad shoulders and dark brown hair climbed out. He waved when he spotted them.

"Hey, Grandpa."

A smile spread over Mr. Connor's face. "Connor," he said. "What brings you out here, young man?"

The passenger-side door opened, and Tyson stepped out. He looked right at Amber and gave her that sheepish grin, and she halted in her tracks.

"Hi," he said, shoving his hands in his pockets.

Mr. Connor looked back and forth between them. "Do you know each other?"

"I don't," Connor said.

"Ms. Morris, this is my grandson, Connor. And this is his friend . . ." Mr. Connor rolled his hand, obviously trying to summon up the name.

"I'm Tyson," he said, and now his grin turned a little more confident. "But Amber knows that already."

Her face burned, and she felt certain the blush would be creeping into her hairline by now. "I was going to call you back," she stammered. "I've just been working. I haven't had the chance yet."

All eyes swiveled to her, and then focused on Tyson. He blinked and then shrugged.

"I wasn't worried."

Of course not. Now she felt even stupider.

"I'm just dropping this off for my mom," Connor said, waving an envelope. "Then we're heading to dinner. You want to come?"

Mr. Connor looked at Amber. "We're done here if you want to go with them. I'll send those estimates over."

What were they talking about? Oh, yes. Estimates. "That sounds great."

"So you'll come to dinner?" Tyson asked, his expression brightening.

"No," Amber said. "I meant the estimates sound great."

"So no dinner." Tyson bobbed his head.

Smokes. She hadn't meant that either. "I didn't mean I wouldn't go to dinner," she blurted. "I mean, I haven't thought about it." Her mind raced, searching for a reason why she couldn't go. It felt too impulsive.

But her parents were home with Raven. There was no reason why she *couldn't* go.

TYSON

Tyson tried to hide his amusement as Amber squirmed, searching for the correct answer to his question. He squinted at her. "So . . . yes to dinner?" He sensed Connor laughing beside him, but when he glanced over, Connor gave him a wide-eyed, innocent expression.

"How about we all go out?" Connor said, stepping up. "I'll call Regina, see if she wants to join us."

Tyson looked back at Amber. "You in?"

"Yes," she said, though she still didn't sound completely in. Her cheeks flushed. "I'll come."

"You sure?" He didn't want her to feel pressured. "You don't have to." She'd obviously had no intention of calling him. If he hadn't run into her just now, they might not have ever spoken again.

Well, until the next wedding at the Crescent.

"No, it's okay. I mean, it's great. Yeah." She took a deep breath.

Like it took a monumental effort to be excited about going to dinner with him.

"Okay." Why was he suddenly so uncertain? You would think he'd never gone out with a girl before. Okay, so it had been a while, but it wasn't a never thing. "Maybe I can get your number now? So I can tell you where we end up going for dinner."

Connor snorted, and it took all Tyson's willpower not to elbow him. Instead he just smiled at Amber, whose face turned even pinker.

"I'll text you," she said. "Then you'll have it."

"You sure you still have my card?"

She opened the satchel across her shoulder and dug into a pocket, then pulled out his card, holding it between her index and middle finger. "Right here. And I have your number on the voicemail at work."

Tyson grinned, pleased beyond words that not only did she still have it, but she knew exactly where it was. Maybe she wasn't going to call him, but she had not forgotten him.

"You should text him right now," Connor said. "So you don't have to worry about it later."

Now Tyson did shoot him a dark look.

"Oh. Right. Okay." Amber pressed a few buttons on her phone, and Tyson's vibrated in his pocket.

"Got it," he said without pulling it out. "I'll call you later."

"Yes. Sounds good." She lifted her hand and gave a small wave, then turned around and headed for her car, clutching her purse to her shoulder and hurrying like someone smelly was on her tail.

Tyson and Connor stood there and watched as she drove away, and then Connor elbowed Tyson hard in the ribs.

"You're welcome," he said.

"Shut up," Tyson said.

♋

Tyson parked his car in front of the Rowdy Beaver. If it was just him and the guys, they would go to the smaller bar on Main Street. But since the girls were coming, they opted for the nicer, full restaurant version.

He spotted Connor and Regina right away, flagging him down at a booth. Tyson jerked his head in greeting while his eyes swept over the people next to them, searching for Amber. She wasn't here yet. She'd texted him her address so he could pick her up, and then she'd changed her mind and said she would meet him here.

She wouldn't stand him up. Right?

Connor stood up and clapped his hand on Tyson's shoulder as he came over. "Ty. She's not here yet."

"I can see that, thanks."

Regina snuggled in close to Connor when he sat, smiling at Tyson. Connor's girlfriend was supermodel gorgeous, with flawless skin, large blue eyes, and straight, blond hair.

"I can't wait to meet your lady friend," Regina said.

"Yeah, well." Tyson ran a hand through his wavy hair. "Let's hope she shows up." He sat down next to Connor and checked his phone. "Is Moki coming?" He stole another glance at his phone screen.

"He said he might come later," Connor said, opening a menu. Regina wrapped her hands around his arm, leaning in close to peer at the menu.

"Gee." Connor gave her an annoyed look and extricated himself. "You have your own menu."

Tyson scrolled through his notifications and pretended not to notice their exchange. Lately it seemed Connor wasn't quite as enamored with Regina as she was with him.

The door opened again, and Tyson stood up when Amber walked in. She had changed out of her black pants and button up shirt, and instead wore a flowing pinstripe brown-and-turquoise dress that looked to be the same shade of blue as her glasses. She looked way too nice for this place.

"Amber!" he called, and she turned his direction, the short brown hair bouncing from one shoulder to the other. She met his eyes and smiled, tucking a strand of hair behind her ear.

Something about her made him want to put her at ease, and Tyson put an arm around her shoulder and guided her into the booth beside him.

"Amber, you've met Connor. That's Regina, his girlfriend."

Amber nodded at everyone, her fingers fumbling with the snap of her purse. Tyson removed his arm from around her shoulders, and she shifted slightly but didn't move away from him.

That had to be a good sign.

They placed their orders for several burgers and fries, and then Regina stood up. Judging from the strapless red dress she wore, Regina and Connor were planning on going somewhere more exciting than the bar after dinner. She shouldered her bag.

"I need to use the ladies' room. Amber, want to come with me?"

"Ah, sure." Amber stood up, shooting Tyson a slightly panicked look that said she was totally out of her element.

He couldn't help her. It wasn't like he could go to the bathroom with them.

"Great." Regina smiled at her and led the way.

Tyson watched the two of them walk away, then he leaned toward Connor. "You guys going somewhere after dinner?"

Connor shrugged, flipping his fork from tines to handle and back again without looking at Tyson. "Gee is always hoping to hit the club."

There was a definite note of bitterness in Connor's voice. Tyson debated ignoring it, then decided Connor wouldn't have made it so obvious unless he wanted to talk about it.

"Something going on with you guys?"

Connor lifted a shoulder again. "I found some messages she was exchanging with this dude she met. She swears it's nothing, but . . ." Connor's voice trailed off.

"You don't trust her," Tyson stated.

"You could say that," Connor said.

"Yeah, but Connor." Tyson shook his head. "You don't trust anyone. Maybe it's not what you think."

"Maybe." But he didn't look any happier about it. "I don't know how you ever get to the point where you can trust a girl enough to want to marry her."

Tyson took a sip of his water and changed the subject. "What do you think of Amber?"

"Too early to say, isn't it?"

That wasn't really the answer Tyson wanted. "She's cute, right?" he pressed.

"For sure," Connor said. "But is she into you?"

"She's here, isn't she?" Tyson said, feeling uncomfortable.

"Yeah, and that says something. But maybe you should give her the chance to show you she's interested. Let her call you next time."

Tyson didn't answer.

"Or ignore me. I'm just trying to watch out for you." Connor raised his eyes to the bathroom. "Here they come."

The girls walked toward the table as one unit, looking more at ease with each other than when they'd gone in. Amber smiled at Tyson as she approached, and he scooted into the booth to make room for her.

"Hi," she said.

"Hi," he replied, bumping her arm with his. "Great to see you here."

"Glad to be here." She picked up her glass and took a sip,

then set it down again. "Thanks for getting me out of the house."

"Anytime."

Chapter Six

AMBER

Nothing exciting or out of the ordinary happened at the Rowdy Beaver with Tyson. She ate, they talked and laughed a bit, and she went home.

His shoulder might have bumped hers more often than was necessary.

And maybe her pinkie finger brushed up against his intentionally.

But was that enough for her to find him invading her thoughts?

Maybe it was because three days had gone by with no word from him.

Friday Amber found herself back at the Crescent Hotel, prepping for a wedding on Saturday. She left Raven with Clarissa and met with the catering staff in the morning. This was her first wedding to do completely on her own, and she wanted it to go perfectly.

"Did you have any problem with anything?" she asked as she looked around the reception hall.

The caterer shook her head. "The tables have been set up as

expected. Everything looks good."

"You don't need anything at all?" Amber searched for a reason why she should go to the front desk and accidentally bump into Tyson.

The caterer looked at her assistant as he smoothed the tablecloth and put another place setting on. He shook his head.

"It's all under control," the caterer said, turning her attention back to Amber. "Your job's easy today."

"Well, that's great. I'll just go thank the hotel management for making sure everything was set up so smoothly."

She shouldered her purse and exited the glass doors, stepping down and continuing straight toward the check-in desk. She saw the same girl working there that Tyson had been talking to last time. She recalled his gentle mannerisms with her, and a nagging doubt filled her mind. Was there something between the two of them? Was that why he hadn't called her?

The girl looked up, and Amber smoothed her features. "Hi. I'm the wedding planner for the Nakamura/Gibbs wedding tomorrow."

"Yes." The girl gave a professional smile. "We have the chapel all arranged for the rehearsal tonight. Anything else you need?"

Is Tyson here? But Amber didn't ask that. She peered over the girl's shoulder, but of course there was nobody hiding behind her at the checkout counter. "No, actually, I just wanted to thank the management for taking such good care of my team."

"Oh." The girl's superficial smile morphed into something more sincere. "I'll pass that along."

Dash it all, Amber would have to be more direct. She took a

deep breath. "Is there anyone from management here?" Amber asked, making one last-ditch, desperate effort to see him.

"Of course. What do you require?"

Amber gave up. Now she would be making a big deal out of nothing. "Nothing. Thank you for your time."

She turned around. As she went back down the corridor, she reached into her purse and retrieved the business card from within the pocket inside. The edges were bending, and the card was no longer pristine white, but Tyson's number was legible.

Not to mention, his number was saved in her phone.

She could always call him.

Amber put the card back with a sigh. She would wait for him to call.

Clarissa arrived like clockwork around six the next morning, and Amber slipped out the door while Raven still slept. The wedding was not for four more hours, but the last hour Amber would spend glued to the bride's side, so this time right now was hers to make sure everything was perfect.

She checked the chapel first. The florist was already on hand. The bride had requested to reuse the flowers, so after the wedding rehearsal the night before, the florist had removed all of the flowers and taken them back to the shop to be refrigerated overnight. The team was here again, putting the same flowers out in new arrangements, rearranging everything and tying ribbons around the bouquets.

"Everything good?" Amber asked, approaching the florist.

"No problems," the woman said, standing back to admire her placement of a bluish-white Asiatic lily. "We always lose a few flowers overnight, but we have more than enough to do the arrangements the bride wanted."

"Fantastic." Confidence rippled up in Amber's chest. So far this wedding was going off without a hitch. It would be another gold star in her portfolio. Violet had to give the promotion to her.

She stayed in the chapel for another twenty minutes, but they didn't need her supervision.

A quick glance at her phone showed it was almost seven. Both the caterer and the bride would be here in an hour. Amber went up to the reception room and checked on the table settings. They looked as pristine as the night before. Amber let out a slow exhale. She had an hour, so she sat down next to the florist and helped tie the ribbons into bows.

She knew the moment the bride arrived from the giggly, loud girly voices that entered the salon accompanied by the squeal of opening doors and clicking heels. Amber stayed in her chair and waited, listening as the hotel staff escorted the bride and her entourage to the room prepared for them. She gave them a good five minutes, enough time to put their things down and gather their bearings but not to feel like they'd been forgotten. Then she put her agenda and notecards away in her satchel and went to the room, replacing her professional smile with a warm, friendly one.

She knocked on the open doorway real quick and stepped inside. "Hi," she said, stepping up to the bride and giving her a hug as if they were friends. Some brides liked the wedding planner to remain aloof and professional, almost clinical, while others wanted someone who felt like a friend, someone who would share the experience with them. Learning to read people and their personalities was part of the job.

Amber stepped back, putting a little more space between them. "How are you feeling today, Akari?"

"Nervous. I'm super excited." Her dark eyes glittered with expectation.

Amber nodded. Her own nerves breathed a figurative sigh of relief. Wedding day jitters she could handle. She hadn't yet had to deal with someone changing their mind on the wedding day, and she hoped she never would.

"You're going to do fantastic today. You have your appointment to get your hair done right now?"

Akari nodded.

"I'll let your bridesmaids tend to you, then. I'm going to check on the caterer, and I'll be back to see you in an hour." Amber flashed her most dazzling smile.

"Thank you." The smile Akari returned was edged with nervousness but radiating happiness.

Amber turned around and walked out, pushing back the familiar twinge in her heart. That was almost her, three years ago, planning her wedding, preparing to spend the rest of her life with the man she loved.

Until she found out she was pregnant. The man she loved never planned for fatherhood. He loved his freedom far more than he loved her or their unborn child.

She shook off the painful reflections as she did at every single wedding. Her life was on the right track, and she could not complain.

She climbed the stairs from the salon back up to the reception room. The caterer had arrived and was setting out the buffet. The hotel staff was there as well, putting tiny bowls with balls of butter on the table. Above each table was suspended a beautiful chain of paper cranes, in honor of the bride's Japanese American heritage. Amber had no skill for origami but had found a woman online who did, and over two hundred cranes danced around the room.

The caterer had laid out the bottom plate for the first layer of the tiered wedding cake. She set the three plastic rods she would need for staging the cake beside the plate. The layers were still carefully cradled in the traveling cake boxes. Amber stepped over to her.

"Need any help here?"

The caterer shook her head without looking up. She smoothed a paper doily over the surface. "I've got this down like clockwork. By the time they come in here for the reception, everything will be out and ready."

"Perfect. I'm just going to—"

An ear-splitting siren rent the air, and the flood lights above the door began to pulse with blinding white lights. Amber clasped her hands over her ears instinctively, but before she could run out of the room to find the cause of the racket, a hissing, spitting noise fought for attention over the shrieking.

Seconds later, water shot out of the overhead sprinkler system.

Every person in the room covered their heads with their arms as if that would prevent them from getting wet. Amber's heart trembled. This could not be happening.

Before she could ask the caterer what they should haul out first, it all stopped. The flashing light, the noise, and the water. She swiveled back around to the caterer.

"Are you okay?"

The woman lifted the lid of one of the boxes, her professional facade slightly shaken. "The cakes are fine. We got lucky." She looked at the doily set up on the stand and ran her finger down the middle of it, bringing up dripping pieces of disintegrating fibers. "Good thing I have more of these papers. But we have to make sure that doesn't happen again, once I pull the cake out . . ."

The woman was still talking, and Amber knew she should pay attention, but for a moment she had stopped breathing. Paper.

All of the cranes.

She whirled around, though she knew what she would see before she did.

The lines still dangled from the ceiling, but instead of hundreds of beautifully formed cranes, globs of wilted paper hung in their place. She choked back a cry. This was a disaster, and there was no way she could replace those cranes in the next hour. Her chest palpitated painfully.

A hotel worker stepped into the room. "I'm so sorry about that." The woman eyed the dripping decor. "What can we do to help?"

Amber gestured at the mess, trying to control her panic. "Can you get this cleaned up?"

"Yes. Right away."

The woman looked uncertain as she backed away, and Amber had no confidence in her.

"Where's the hotel manager?" she demanded.

"Mr. Hafford?"

"Yes!" Amber snapped, and then she took a deep breath, struggling for control.

"I called him right away. It's his day off, but he should be here any moment."

Tyson was on his way. He would fix this. He had to do something.

"I'll get someone in here to start cleaning up." The woman hurried away.

Amber turned to face the room, feeling overwhelmed. Where to start? She climbed on a table and started removing the cranes as a man came in with a mop and a bucket.

"Is everyone okay in here?" Tyson stepped into the room, dressed in jeans and a button-up shirt and looking harried. He was still in the process of attaching the radio to his hip. "I'm so sorry—"

Amber launched herself at him. "What was that? There had bloody well have been a fire because this wedding is ruined!" She blinked rapidly, forcing back the burning tears.

His eyes widened slightly when he saw her, and then they swept around the room. "There was a small fire in the kitchen. It set off the alarms in the entire hotel. I came right away. How can I help?"

Think rationally. Amber struggled to get herself under control. "You can't fix this. You can issue an official apology to the bride. I'll take it from there."

She spun on her heel, ready to yank down all of the lines, but Tyson stepped out and grabbed her arm.

"I'm really sorry," he said, his eyes searching hers. "Let me help. What was ruined?"

She pulled free of his arm and stepped to the first line of paper cranes. She stood on a chair and then on the table. Not caring if her shoe poked into the wet tablecloth, she pulled out a line of deceased cranes. She handed it to him, watching the confusion on his face as he fingered the sopping paper.

"Origami," she supplied. "Hundreds of paper cranes decorated this room in honor of the bride's cultural heritage." The bite had left her tone. Logically she knew this wasn't the hotel's fault, and it definitely wasn't Tyson's; sprinklers were a safety precaution for fires.

Tyson stared at them, and then his expression lit up. "Give me two hours. I can fix this."

She stared at him in bewilderment. "How? Are you a closet origamist?"

"No." He handed the line back to her. "I'll get my people cleaning up in here. You take care of the bride. Don't worry about this."

With that he walked out, hand pressing a button on his radio as he began to bark orders.

TYSON

Connor didn't pick up his phone the first time Tyson called, and he was in too big a hurry to call again. He careened away from the hotel, taking the switch-back curves a little too fast as he hurried downtown. He'd made a promise to Amber, and he couldn't fail her now.

Trying to find a parking spot on Spring Street took nearly ten minutes, and Tyson finally parked at an empty meter, which he loaded a few quarters into before rushing down the sidewalk to Connor's mom's shop.

Tyson might not be a closet origamist, but he was pretty sure he knew where to find one.

The bell chimed when he walked in, and Tyson took in the eclectic surroundings before looking toward Connor, who was helping an old lady wrap up several tea cups. The antique shop was a crazy mix of old and new. Connor glanced up long enough to see him, then he returned his attention to the lady.

"Let me put these in a box for you so they don't shift while you drive. Here you go. Thank you for your business." He moved from behind the counter and opened the door for her.

Tyson watched her shuffle down the sidewalk before facing Connor. "I need help."

"What is it?"

"I need someone who can do origami. And fast."

Connor arched one eyebrow. "You need someone who can do origami fast?"

"No. Well, yes, that too. But I need someone fast. As in, right now. Who do you know?"

Connor went back behind the counter and pulled out a stack of business cards. "Let me check."

Tyson grinned, some of his panic subsiding. Of course Connor had someone. Connor kept tabs on all kinds of artists, especially those with an unusual skill that he might have need of later.

"This guy can probably help." Connor removed a card and squinted at it.

Tyson stepped forward and snatched the card. Akemi Yamamoto. "Great. I'll call him right now."

He didn't even leave Connor's store to place the call.

The guy answered on the second ring. "Hello?"

"Hey," Tyson said, aware of Connor watching him. "I got your number from Connor Thompson. He's a friend of mine. Says you do origami?"

"Yes," the guy said, and now Tyson heard the slightest hint of an accent. "What do you need?"

"I need cranes. You do cranes?"

Akemi laughed. "Everyone does cranes."

"Can you make me two hundred in two hours?"

"No."

"In two and a half hours?"

"No."

"I'll pay you," Tyson said, growing desperate. "A lot of money."

"Cranes cannot be rushed."

"What if we helped?" Connor said.

Great idea. "Connor and I can help. The three of us can

make that many."

"Why do you need so many so fast?"

"It's for a wedding. That's happening in three hours."

Akemi sighed loudly. "I'll have to rearrange my schedule, but I can come to Mr. Thompson's store. It is going to cost you, though."

"I know. Thank you." Tyson hung up the phone and took a deep breath.

"Guess we're making cranes?"

Tyson shot Connor a crooked smile. "You offered."

"I'm also guessing this has something to do with Amber?"

He nodded. "The cranes for the wedding were ruined when the sprinkler system went off. Stupid old hotel. I thought she would cry. If I can fix this for her—"

"You'll be her knight in shining armor." Connor smirked. "Has she called you yet?"

"How dare you ask such a degrading question," Tyson growled, which only made Connor laugh.

Connor locked the shop and put up the closed sign while the three of them worked. First Akemi spent ten minutes instructing them on how to create the cranes, then they set to work. Akemi's cranes were uniform, elegant, and came to life quickly, while Tyson cringed if he looked too closely at the misshapen, oddly sized cranes he and Connor made.

But after two hours they had two hundred. And Tyson had two hundred dollars less in his wallet.

"Good luck," Akemi said as he pocketed the money.

"Yeah," Connor said, his eyes laughing. "Good luck with your wedding."

"It's your wedding?" Akemi stopped his movement.

Tyson wanted to shoot Connor. "No."

"Oh." Akemi flashed a smile. "I would give you a discount if it were. Have a nice day."

Connor only managed to contain his laughter until Akemi walked out, and then it burst out of him. "You should have said yes."

"You're terrible."

"I just spent two hours making cranes with you."

"I owe you."

"Go impress your woman."

"I will." Tyson picked up the large box of cranes and pushed his way out of the store.

Amber was nowhere in sight when he returned to the hotel. Music drifted from the chapel just below the building, and his heart raced with anxiety. He didn't have a lot of time. He pressed the button on his radio and summoned all his available workers to the reception hall.

"All right," he mumbled, pulling out the line used for the cranes. "Let's do this."

It took twenty minutes with ten employees helping him, and when Tyson stepped back to admire their handiwork, he fought hard not to wince. Large and frumpy birds danced on the line beside sleek, beautiful cranes. He could easily pick out the ones he and Connor had made compared to the ones Akemi had done.

But time was up. There was nothing he could do about it now. He cleared his mess out, leaving the reception hall prepped and ready for the caterers and the wedding party.

He hoped it was good enough.

Chapter Seven

AMBER

Tyson hadn't stuck around after the sprinklers went off. He barked orders into his radio and left.

She resented him for it, even though he didn't leave her alone, and even though he promised he could fix this. She was wounded that he hadn't called her, and now he'd assigned his staff to clean up the mess without saying another word to her.

His staff immediately began the cleanup process. Within minutes, the wet tablecloths had been stripped and replaced with dry ones, and new pads of butter with dry napkins and polished silverware set out. Amber watched for a moment until she was certain they did not require her supervision, and then she hurried downstairs to the salon to check on the bride. Her heart sank at the thought that the sprinklers might've destroyed any makeup or hairstyle the stylist had accomplished.

The floors were dry downstairs. Amber found the bride in the same room as before, except this time her hair was full of rollers and two different women worked on her makeup. She looked into the mirror and caught Amber's eye.

Before Amber could apologize for the commotion, Akari asked, "What happened? It sounded like a fire alarm went off."

"Did it not go off down here?"

Akari shook her head. "We could hear it from here, so we wondered about it."

The makeup artist turned the chair so Amber could look at the bride. "How does her face look?"

Akari was already stunning, but the heavier black eyeliner around her almond eyes emphasized her Asian background. With the red lipstick against her porcelain skin, she looked like a movie star.

"You look priceless," Amber said, and her heart tumbled with relief that the sprinkler system had not gone off down here.

The relief must have been evident on her face, because the bride lifted an eyebrow and asked, "Is everything okay up there?"

Amber debated telling her about the ruined paper cranes, but she crossed her mental fingers that Tyson could really pull through like he'd promised. "Oh, everything is fine. No problem upstairs. None at all." *We didn't just throw water on two-hundred delicate origami cranes.* She stretched her face into a wide smile, crinkling the skin under her eyes for effect. Then she dropped it and left the room before it became apparent she was totally bluffing.

She let out a deep breath and smoothed her skirt, her body temperature rising as if it knew it was crunch time. She told herself there was nothing to do except wait for Tyson to come back, but she was too anxious to be still. Amber went to the chapel and checked on the flowers and ceremony officials.

Then she returned to the reception hall.

Other than the missing cranes, no one would ever guess there'd been a problem. The caterer had finished setting up the wedding cake, and the exquisite cherry blossom decorations coupled with the Western wedding figurines was the perfect blend of the two cultures.

The caterer tied a bow at the front of the cake and saw Amber. "Just as long as it doesn't sprinkle on us now."

Amber shook her head, doing her best to give a confident smile. "That won't happen again." She crossed her mental fingers that her statement would be correct.

She made the rounds one more time, checking her watch excessively. No sign of Tyson.

It would be what it would be. It was time to start gathering people in. She would just have to explain to the bride after the ceremony that there'd been a hitch.

Sometimes it happened. But Amber regretted it. She wanted this wedding to be perfect for Akari.

The bride had moved to the chapel after her hair and makeup were done so she could put on her dress and get the finishing touches applied. Amber hurried past the open front door, listening to the excited chatter of wedding guests.

Amber let herself in through the back door and went straight to the dressing room.

Akari stood in a circle of bridesmaids, and she handed out small bracelets as a thank you to each one of them.

"You are my most favorite people in all the world and it makes me the happiest person ever to share this day with you."

Her friends gasped and hugged her, some of them crying.

"Don't you dare cry," one of them said. "You don't want to

ruin that exquisite makeup."

The photographer snapped a few pictures and cleared her throat. "We have about ten minutes. Let's move down to the hallway and wait for our cue from the organist."

A hush settled over them, and a look of radiant expectation that Amber had come to recognize brushed over Akari's features. Amber couldn't help the smile that touched her lips. This woman was happy because she was marrying the man she loved. She probably would not even notice the missing cranes.

They were in position when the music began, and each person made their way down the aisle in the order expected. There were no further surprises, and the wedding ceremony was picture-book perfect.

Amber's stomach knotted up again as soon as it finished. Now for the reception. She slipped out of the chapel and hurried across the parking lot, uttering prayers that everything would be going smoothly in the reception hall. She stepped in the back doors to the hotel and walked through the entry hall before swinging a left toward the reception hall. She pushed open the doors, her eyes immediately sweeping toward the long table with the beautiful cake—and she drew up short.

Cranes.

More cranes than she could count dangled above each table like a delicate chandelier. They came in a variety of colors and sizes, not nearly as uniform and symmetrical as her original white cranes, but they were just as beautiful and inspiring in their kaleidoscope.

An unfamiliar heady and intoxicating feeling swelled in her chest. Tyson. How had he done this? And why? Why go through all this effort for her? Maybe he was only doing his job, but somehow this felt more personal.

The wedding party approached, noisy in their giddy chatter and exuberance. Amber quieted her emotions to focus on her work. She would find Tyson and thank him as soon as she had a quiet moment.

TYSON

Tyson didn't see Amber during the reception. He heard the noise from the wedding group and wanted to spy on them, make sure everything was going well. But he also didn't want to get in the way, so he found a list of small repairs from the owner and made himself busy.

When the parents of the bride and groom slipped outside to decorate the getaway car, Tyson followed them.

"Excuse me," he said, stepping up to a woman with dark hair and Asian features similar to those of the bride. "Are you the mother of the bride?"

"Yes," she said, turning to him with a glowing smile. She radiated happiness, which Tyson took to be a good sign.

"I wanted to apologize for the sprinkler incident earlier. We pride ourselves on providing a perfect venue for every event, and we're so sorry something went wrong. I've worked with the wedding planner to provide a complimentary honeymoon suite for the married couple any time within the next year."

The woman's eyes went wide with surprise. "Sprinkler incident?"

She didn't even know. That meant he'd fixed it well enough that no one noticed. "We had a kitchen fire, and the subsequent noise may have alarmed your daughter. Even if it didn't, I'd like to offer the suite as an apology."

"Oh, that's very kind of you! I'm sure they would love to take advantage of that when they return from their honeymoon."

Tyson nodded. "That sounds great. Stop by the front desk before you leave and I'll get it all set up for you."

"Thank you for everything. The wedding, the venue, it was all perfect. Ms. Morris is an amazing wedding planner. I can't recommend her enough. The two of you make a good team."

"Well." Tyson's face grew hot, and he nodded, backing away. "She's—yep." No need to wax lyrical and extol Amber's virtues to this lady. "I look forward to talking with you later." He turned and took the steps two at a time before ducking into the office to let his face cool off.

He wanted to talk to Amber, but when Tyson checked the schedule, the reception hall was reserved for two more hours. She wouldn't be available until after. He didn't have any other reason to hang out around the hotel. He sent her a quick text before heading out.

Sorry again about the sprinklers. Hope all went well. He paused. Should he tell her he'd call her? Invite her out to dinner?

Was that too presumptuous when she hadn't shown any indication of wanting to hang out again?

Talk later, he finished. Then he sent the message off, grabbed his keys, and left.

AMBER

Amber stayed at the hotel until the last wedding accessory had been cleaned up and put away. She checked for Tyson at the front desk, but Jaya said he'd already gone home. Amber had suspected as much when she got his text message, but she'd been too occupied to search him out.

Which meant there was nothing left for Amber to do but go home also. A giddy contentedness hummed through her soul, vibrating into her shoulders as she drove on the twisty roads.

Raven ran to hug Amber the moment she walked in the door, and Amber did a quick check to make sure she didn't have any raspberry jam on her hands before picking up her daughter.

"Thanks for watching her," she said to Clarissa, pulling out her wallet and handing over several bills.

"No problem. Do you need me next Saturday also?" The girl pocketed the bills and lifted her face to Amber's.

"Yes. That would be great." Raven snuggled her head into Amber's neck.

Clarissa smiled. "Okay. Let me know if something comes up tomorrow. I've got an appointment in the morning, but I'm free in the afternoon." She tilted her head. "You seem a little . . . strange. Something going on?"

Amber couldn't help the heat that rushed up to her cheeks. "No . . . Not really."

"There is something," Clarissa said, her smile becoming more knowing.

"Okay," Amber said, grabbing Clarissa's arm. "I've got the day off tomorrow. I wanted to take Raven to the children's museum in Bentonville. Come with us. I'll pay you to keep an eye on her and tell you everything."

Clarissa waved her off. "You can't pay me to hang out with you."

Amber laughed. "I'll buy you lunch, then."

"I accept. See you tomorrow."

Even though there had been plenty of food at the wedding, Amber had been too nervous to eat. The peanut butter and jelly were still out from Raven's lunch, so Amber fixed herself a sandwich and settled down in front of The Food Network, carrying on her father's tradition in spite of herself.

But she didn't really focus on the food. Her thoughts kept going back to Tyson, to the way he stepped in and saved her, the determined look on his face when he realized the trouble she was in. It wasn't a life-threatening incident, and it wasn't even his fault.

The question was, why had he done it? Was it really just because it was his job?

Whatever the reason, he deserved a thank you.

She fished her phone out of her bag and hesitated only a moment before opening a message to him. *Thank you for your help today. You really pulled through.* There was more she could say, more she was thinking, but she didn't want to assume too much. So she sent the message off.

It was only moments later that she got a response. *Happy to help. Glad it worked out. Here if you need anything.*

She pondered that last sentence, trying to interpret it. It sounded like something a friend would say, the whole "you can rely on my friendship." Or was he hinting at more? And if so, what?

You're reading too much into it, she told herself. *All he means is that anytime you're doing a wedding at the Crescent Hotel, he will be there to make sure it goes smoothly.*

A crash sounded from the kitchen, followed by the tinkling of something shattering all over the floor. Amber leapt to her feet and dashed from the room. "Raven?"

There was no response from the little girl, and Amber picked up her pace. Her eyes quickly scanned the kitchen until she found her daughter, sitting on top of the counter on her hands and knees with a guilty expression on her face. Then Amber's eyes flew to the kitchen floor, where the fruit bowl lay in shards, bruised and split apples around it.

"Raven!" Amber exclaimed. "How could you do this?" Her great-grandmother's heirloom crystal bowl was no more. She grabbed Raven by the forearm and yanked her off the counter. Amber set her on the safety of the carpeted living room floor before giving her bum a swat.

Raven immediately opened her mouth and wailed like a banshee.

"Go to your room while I clean up this mess!" Amber ordered, trying hard to keep her fury under control. When Raven just stood there, she shouted, "Go!"

Raven gave her a look of absolute sadness. Tears streamed down her face as she dashed to her bedroom, and guilt slashed through Amber. She sat down on the floor next to the shattered glass and put her face in her hands. She didn't mean to lose her temper. She wanted to be fair and understanding, but sometimes this mothering thing was just so hard.

She wiped her face and cleaned up the glass, using a vacuum to make sure she got all the tiny pieces.

Raven's cries had stopped from the bedroom, and Amber tiptoed inside to check on the little girl. She'd fallen asleep on her bed, soft hiccups still escaping her mouth. Amber patted back the black curls and pressed a kiss to Raven's temple.

"I'm not mad, baby," she whispered. "I'm sorry. Be patient with me."

Raven didn't wake or respond, of course, but Amber hoped somehow she knew Amber's heart.

The next morning, Amber loaded Raven up in the car and made the trip to Bentonville. It was a pleasant drive, slow as they took the switchback curves out of the mountainous region of Eureka Springs and into the flatter, calmer terrain in the city district of Bentonville. Perfect for a Sunday morning.

The children's museum was always busy on the weekend, and Amber had to drive across the street to the Crystal Bridges art museum just to find a spot. Then she tucked Raven into the stroller before pushing them back over to the museum.

The sign out front said the special exhibit was on trees, but first Amber had to get through the long line of patrons trying to get in. Raven spotted other children playing with the cloud machine and chasing each other around their parents. She fussed to get free, but Amber wouldn't relent, glad she'd buckled Raven in so she couldn't run.

They made it through the line, and only after they'd bypassed the crowds and made it to the log cabin in the back of the museum did she let Raven out. She settled into a rocking chair and heaved a sigh, glad to have nothing to do right now except watch her daughter play.

Clarissa arrived an hour later, when they'd moved past the log cabin to the indoor water area.

"This is kind of cool," she said, sidling up to Raven. "I've never been in here before."

"Oh!" Amber exclaimed. "I was going to pay your entry fee."

Clarissa waved her off. "I'm having fun. It's no biggie."

Amber relented, letting Clarissa have that one. Clarissa might have started out as a babysitter, but the two girls became fast friends, and sometimes it was difficult to separate business from friendship. Clarissa constantly tried to take less pay for watching Raven, claiming it was her privilege as honorary aunt, but it reminded Amber too much of how her parents had taken care of Raven for free while Amber finished college.

Raven ran over to them, soaking wet in spite of the yellow poncho she wore and giggling like a mad man. She threw her arms around Clarissa's legs, then turned to Amber.

"Outside?"

"Yes," Amber said, laughing. The hot July sun would help dry her off.

Amber and Clarissa settled down on one of the benches, trying to stay in the shade while Raven played in the little house by the fish pond.

Clarissa turned her attention to Amber. "So? What's new?"

Amber shrugged. "Absolutely nothing. I'm just a boring mom."

Clarissa swatted Amber's arm. "Don't you dare let yourself think that way. You're still young and gorgeous and have so much life in front of you. Don't start thinking you're some old maid."

Amber laughed. She kept an eye on Raven to make sure she didn't climb the roof of the house. "How is your class at NWACC going?"

"Pretty good, I guess. It's art history. We're focusing on the Greeks right now, and their appreciation of art is very different from mine. But you didn't invite me to the children's museum to talk about my class."

"No," Amber said, her face somehow getting even hotter. "I didn't."

Clarissa stared at her, waiting, but Amber couldn't seem to find the words to say it. She took a deep breath, cleared her throat, and then said, "I think I might like someone."

Clarissa's mouth dropped open. "No. Way."

"Yeah." Amber wiped at her forehead. "I keep running into him at work. And I can't stop thinking about him."

"But you're scared," Clarissa said.

"I don't know if scared is the right word," Amber said, frowning. "I'm cautious."

"You can like a guy, Amber. You won't get pregnant from that."

"But dating leads to other things," Amber murmured, pulling on the angel charm on her necklace.

"So be careful," Clarissa said, a smile playing about her lips. "You're already thinking about sex with this guy?"

Amber didn't deign to answer the question. "I was careful last time. And I still got pregnant."

Clarissa pulled her hand away from the necklace and forced Amber to meet her eyes. "You were going to marry Drake. If he hadn't decided he didn't want to be a dad, you would've had a shotgun wedding, had Raven, and be living happily ever after together. Getting pregnant wasn't the tragedy. Being abandoned was."

The truth in the words stung, and Amber swallowed against a lump in her throat. "So what I need to do before I trust a guy with all of my heart and hopes and dreams is make sure I know who he really is."

Amber's phone dinged, and she picked it up, grateful for the distraction. Hopefully it wasn't a client with some emergency. Ava was handling today's wedding and wouldn't ask for Amber's help even if she needed it.

Her heart gave a surprised little tumble when she saw Tyson's name.

Hey. What are you doing today?

She read the text message, trying to match his voice to the words. Was he serious when he wrote this, that intense look in his eyes as he focused on a task? Or was he a little shy, that sheepish grin playing at the corner of his mouth?

"Amber."

Amber jerked her head up to see Clarissa staring at her, one eyebrow lifted.

"You have the goofiest grin on your face." Clarissa said each word emphatically. "Tell me that text was from him."

Amber pressed her lips together, but she couldn't keep the smile off them. "Yes."

"You have to tell me everything."

"I just met him a few weeks ago. We've been talking. But he's . . . he's sweet. And thoughtful. And professional. And he goes the extra mile to make sure I have what I need." His face popped into her mind again, the mischievous glint in his eyes, the wavy brown hair, the cute little smile. "And he's really cute."

"Seriously? He can't be as perfect as all that."

"No. No, of course not. Nobody's perfect." And yet, everything she'd seen of Tyson was pretty close. She recognized the yearning in her heart. She wanted to spend time with him. She wanted to see if he was as genuine as he appeared. She hoped he was.

"But you're not dating?"

Amber shook her head. "No. We're still just getting to know each other."

"Are you avoiding dating him because you don't want to sleep with him? Because you know you don't have to sleep with him just because you're dating. You can always say no. You don't even have to give an explanation. That's your right."

Amber rolled her eyes. "Thanks for the vote of confidence."

"I don't want you to miss out dating this guy that you obviously really like because you're afraid it will go too far." She shrugged. "Who knows? Maybe you'll even want it to."

Amber gave a short laugh. "It's never a matter of not wanting to."

They both giggled at that, and for a moment Amber felt more carefree, more like the young woman she was instead of the matronly mother she felt like.

"So what did his text say?" Clarissa asked, inclining her head toward the phone.

Amber picked it up and read through it again. "He just wants to know what I'm doing today."

"What are you going to tell him?"

Before Amber could answer, her phone rang. Her heart leapt into her throat when she saw his name scrolling over the screen. "He's calling me."

Clarissa grinned. "You took too long to respond."

Amber stood up and answered the phone, moving closer the

brick wall and putting some space between her and Clarissa. "Hello?"

"Hey. Amber?" Tyson's rich tenor voice carried through the line, and something inside Amber's stomach tightened.

"Yeah, hey."

"Sorry, I hope I'm not bothering you, I just wasn't sure if you saw my text."

"I did."

"Oh." There was a pause. "Well, sorry. I . . ."

His voice trailed off, and Amber realized he thought her lack of response meant his communication was not well received. She interrupted him, anxious to put him at ease.

"You're fine. I was just talking with a friend and didn't get a chance to respond."

"I don't want to interrupt."

This wasn't going the direction Amber wanted it to. He had asked what she was doing for a reason, and she wanted to pursue that thought. "What are you doing today?"

"Well. Some friends and I are going to the lake. I thought I'd see if you wanted to come, but looks like you've got plans."

"I'm in Bentonville," Amber said. Her mind scrambled to figure out how quickly she could get to the lake from here.

And then she remembered Raven. Her heart sank. She couldn't just stop and go anywhere. She had a little girl to take care of.

Clarissa waved both hands back and forth, trying to get Amber's attention.

"Well," Tyson said slowly, as of thinking while he spoke, "we'll be out here all day. You could bring your friend too."

Clarissa was on her feet now, waving madly.

"Hang on." Amber removed the phone from her ear and pressed it to her chest. "What?"

"Does he want to do something with you?"

"He does, but . . ." Amber shrugged one shoulder. "I'm here with you. And I've got Raven."

"Go. Raven's fine." Clarissa gestured to the black-haired toddler playing in the sandbox. "I'll take her to your house when she gets bored here."

"No." Amber said the word without hesitation. She would not take advantage of Clarissa's friendship.

"Oh, please." Clarissa rolled her eyes. "You can buy me dinner or something. You're wasting time. Tell him you'll go. And make sure you leave me the car seat."

A spark of excitement flared in Amber's chest. Could she really? Could she go on a date with him and just be young and carefree for an afternoon?

Clarissa was nodding her head up and down, answering her unspoken question.

Amber cleared her throat and lifted the phone back to her ear. "You know what, my friend can't come, but I would love to. Where are you? I have to go home and get a change of clothes, so it will probably be like two hours."

"Hey, that's totally fine." A rich note of pleasure had entered Tyson's voice, and she could imagine the smile that would light his face. "Text me when you're ready, and I'll give you directions."

"Okay." Amber hung up the phone and gave a little squeal. She pressed her hands to her cheeks. "Oh my goodness! I don't remember the last time I was this nervous."

"He must really be something."

The image of hundreds of multicolored cranes dangling through the ceiling flashed through Amber's mind. "I think he might be."

TYSON

"You sure you can't get the boat today?" Tyson followed Connor and Moki to the Connor Landscaping work truck, where Connor dumped several paddles next to the four kayaks he'd shoved into the back.

"Can't. Dave said he needs it." Connor said it flatly, and Tyson knew he'd be pushing his luck if he asked again.

"But it's the perfect day for it. And everyone's going to be at the lake," Moki whined. Apparently he hadn't picked up on Connor's tone.

"Yep. And we can kayak or hang out on the beach. Those are our options." He opened the truck door. "You coming or not?"

"After you." Tyson gestured Moki forward.

Only once they were inside did Moki complain, "Hey! I'm stuck in the middle!"

Connor and Tyson both laughed.

The beach area at Lake Leatherwood was dotted with scantily clothed bodies, towels, paddle boats, and inflatable devices.

"There." Connor parked in front of a pavilion. "There's Regina. She's already got the grill going."

Moki whistled. "She's hot. You're lucky she's devoted to

you."

Regina had her blond hair pulled into a side ponytail and wore cut off shorts with a bikini top. Tyson exchanged a look with Connor and knew they both questioned Regina's devotion. But he didn't say anything.

Several other people crowded the pavilion with Regina, kids Tyson recognized from high school and around town. He grabbed the cooler of drinks from the back of the truck and dragged it to the pavilion, greeting the coconut-scented crowd. He glanced back at the parking lot every two seconds, watching for Amber and her little blue Civic.

"Ty!"

Tyson turned his head when Monica Williams planted herself on the bench beside him. Her curly brown hair was pulled into pigtails, and her button up shirt was tied just above her belly button.

"Monica, hey." He arched an eyebrow in surprise. Monica had been his high school crush, but she'd always brushed him off as insignificant.

"Oh, it's been so long!" She wrapped her hand around his biceps and leaned forward as if giving him some kind of push-up hug. "You look fantastic! What are you up to these days? I never see you!"

Tyson blinked, a flurry of unexpected emotions rising up in him. He waited for excitement, or eagerness, but . . . that one wasn't there. Only nervousness, and anxiety that Amber might see her and think there was more than met the eye. "Oh, you know. The usual. Working. Sleeping. Eating."

"Yeah? Where are you working?"

At that moment, the blue Civic Tyson had been waiting for pulled into a spot across the street. Tyson jumped to his feet, and he noted how he'd rather spend his time with Amber than

Monica. "My girlfriend's here. We'll catch up another time, Monica."

"Oh! Yeah. Sure."

Tyson didn't stop to analyze the look on Monica's face. Amber was getting out of her car. She had reached across the driver's seat to get something on the passenger side, and he jogged over.

"Hey," he said when she turned around. He put his hands on her waist and pulled her in for a hug. He wasn't sure if that was being too presumptuous, but Monica was watching.

"Hi," she replied, sounding surprised. But she wrapped her arms around his neck and returned the hug.

Oh. Now he didn't wanna let go. She smelled good, like honey and lemons. He squeezed her harder and then forced himself to release her before he did something foolish, like kiss her.

"I didn't expect that," she said with a little laugh. She shouldered a bag with a rolled towel hanging out of it.

"You should have." He took her bag from her, even though it didn't weigh much.

"I can carry that," she protested.

"Just because you can doesn't mean you should." He held his hand out to her, and a ripple of delight flooded him when she took it.

She didn't hold on for long, though. Once they reached the pavilion and he began to introduce her, she let go, pleating her hands together in front of her and smiling anxiously.

"Hot dogs are done," Regina called out. "Burgers will be a bit longer."

"Hot dogs or burgers?" Tyson asked Amber.

"I'll take a burger."

"Then we have some time. Come on, let's swim."

He half expected her to decline, but she looked out at the water and said, "Okay."

His fingers glided between hers naturally this time as they walked to the lake. Here the single crowd gave way to families with small children building rock castles and loading up buckets of water. Tyson sat down close enough to the shore to dip his feet in the water and dig his fingers in the damp sand. Amber put her towel next to him and settled onto it. She had removed her sundress, and her fair skin already showed signs of color through the streaks of sunscreen.

"How do you know those guys?" she asked, bobbing her head at the pavilion behind them.

"You live here long enough, you meet everyone. College, high school, preschool."

"Well, great. I plan to be here a while, so soon I'll have lots of friends."

"Yeah, people are friendly here. Very accepting."

"You are, anyway."

Tyson didn't know what to say to that, other than, how could he resist a cute girl like her? So he stayed quiet. He gathered up piles of dirt mixed with sand and mounded them together, his lame attempt at a sandcastle. "What brought you to Eureka?"

"Violet. I met her in Fayetteville when I was working a wedding, and she told me she could offer me better opportunities if I came here. So I did. And you? Why are you working at the hotel? Did you major in business economics or something?"

"Nothing as exciting as that. I majored in philosophy with the intent to go to law school. Somehow I haven't managed to send in an application yet."

She lay back on her towel, resting on her elbows, and looked at him. "Why?"

He cocked a brow and opted for a perplexed expression. "The application fees are a lot of money?"

She humored him with a brief smile. "Are you afraid you won't get in? Or are you having second thoughts about being a lawyer?"

"It's complicated and it's not. Yeah, I'm afraid of failure. My mom always said I couldn't make a decision to save my life, and I guess it's true. I've been planning on law school for years and can't seem to hit the submit button. And then what? What if I actually get in somewhere and go to school and I don't like it? What if I finish school and don't pass the bar? What if I pass the bar and get my license only to find I'm not interested in being a lawyer after all? That really all I wanted to do was accrue massive amounts of debt so that I could work behind a hotel check-in desk for the rest of my life?"

Her look was gentle this time, full of understanding. "Those are a lot of fears."

Tyson looked back out over the lake, surprised he had opened up to her that easily. "My mom also said I wouldn't amount to anything."

"Shame on her. And shame on you for believing her."

He turned his face to look at her.

"Your mother should've been your biggest supporter. She should've encouraged your dreams. So that's on her. But you are your own person now, a grown man with the ability to shape your own future. So that's on you."

Her eyes shown with passion. Her mouth captivated him, and Tyson found himself leaning closer without meaning to. "You're right," he said. "I've got no one to blame but myself for holding back."

Her eyes held his even as he leaned closer. "So what's

stopping you now?"

"Nothing." He dipped his face to hers and kissed her, pressing his lips gently against hers. He pulled back long enough to check her expression, gauge her reaction. She gave him a small smile, her cheeks flushed, just enough permission for Tyson to lean in and kiss her again. "Absolutely nothing."

The party at the lake migrated to Tyson's house in the evening, with the majority of people bailing. Tyson's house, with the expansive front yard and the game room in the basement, was the perfect location for a big group.

Not that Tyson cared. Amber came along, and that was all that mattered.

He made a conscious choice not to hang on her at the lake. He wanted to touch her, keep his hand on hers, stake his claim. But more than that, he didn't want her to feel suffocated. He felt the electric charge between them every time he was near her, and he might have bumped her arm a time or two, but mostly he let the attraction he felt for her build by not allowing himself to give into it.

She stayed by his side in his house, opening up cupboards and finding the disposable cups, then filling a bowl with ice cubes and setting out food on the counter. The guests made themselves at home, turning on the television and lounging across the chairs.

"Want to play pool?" Tyson asked Amber.

"Sure," she said. "But I'm gonna warn you now, I'm pretty good."

"Then let me just reassure you. So am I." He smirked at her and touched her knuckles before turning for the stairs. He heard her laughter and felt her walking behind him. Every muscle on his body attuned itself to her, wanting to narrow the distance between them.

The basement had a few people in it, also, the television blaring as his guests argued over what to watch. Moki had a pool game going already, and Tyson handed Amber a cue.

"Can we join you?" he asked Moki.

"You'll be at a disadvantage."

"Not for long," Amber said, and the boys hooted. A few girls leaned against the table, also, but they eyed Amber up like she was competition rather than a potential ally.

More like the victor. But they'd know that soon enough.

Amber caught Tyson off guard in the first game, beating all of them by more than sixty points. But by the second game, he had his war face on. He would have beaten her, too, if Moki hadn't bumped his arm and made him hit the eight-ball.

"Do-over," Amber said, setting the balls up. "For your sake."

"I don't need a pity game," Tyson said.

"Yes, you do." She smirked up at him, her eyes alluring behind the frames. "Prove you can do this."

Can I just kiss you instead? he thought, but he managed to keep it to himself. "I'll show you."

"I'm waiting."

"Stay back, Moki."

"I'm totally out of the way."

It was only him and Amber this time, with the others stepping back to watch the standoff. Tyson let his competitive nature come out, and he concentrated hard on his strategy and aim. But something about the way that brown-eyed girl watched him was disarming, and she beat him again.

"We have a new champion!" Moki crowed, grabbing Amber's arm and lifting it high above her head. "Hand over your crown, Tyson!"

"I'll have to find it later. If I don't win back my title before then."

"You can try anytime." Amber beamed at him.

Most of the party had left by now. Amber pulled out her phone and checked the time, a frown creasing her forehead.

"I should probably go now."

"Really?" Tyson checked his own phone. "It's not even ten yet." He'd hoped she'd be one of the last people to leave so he could be alone with her.

"Yeah, well." She shrugged. "I didn't plan to be gone all day."

"No, of course not." He swallowed back his disappointment and cursed the crowd of people who had followed him to his house. He glared at Moki, who seemed oblivious to the laser-eyes. "I'll walk you to your car." He put the pool cues away while she waited, then they walked up the stairs and through the main part of the house.

Only after Tyson closed the front door behind them did the noise of other voices die down. Instead, the chirping of crickets and the singing of the cicadas greeted them. She slowed down on the walkway, allowing him to catch up to her.

"Sorry I have to go," she said, and she sounded genuine. "I had a great time."

"Did you?" He reached out and took her hand, almost sighing in relief as his skin finally touched hers again. He threaded his fingers through hers. "I hope I didn't keep you from anything important."

She stopped at her car and faced him, her hand still locked with his. "I really enjoyed being with you. And I'm serious about what I said earlier. It's your time."

He knew she referenced his law school application, but his

heart did a little jump in his chest, and he didn't think it had anything to do with law school. He drew nearer and kissed her again, softly touching her mouth with his. His heart rate ratcheted up, a euphoric mixture of panic and ecstasy flooding his mind. He used his hold on her hand to pull her closer, his other arm going around her back and cradling her to him. His body responded to her nearness, but when he tried to deepen the kiss, she tilted her head back and turned just enough that his lips met her cheek. Then she stepped off the curb, withdrawing from his embrace and freeing her hand.

He felt her absence and desperately wanted to bring her back. But he also recognized when a line was being drawn, and he hoped he hadn't accidentally crossed one.

"Good night, Tyson," she said.

"Night, Amber," he echoed. He put a hand on her car door as she opened it. "I'll call you tomorrow?" His heart was in those words, begging her to tell him she wanted to see him again.

"I hope so." She shot him a shy smile from the driver's seat, too shy for someone who had just been kissing him.

Yet it reassured him. They were both hesitant, nervous here.

"Talk to you tomorrow, then." He stepped back to the sidewalk and waved as she drove away.

Chapter Nine

AMBER

Amber dropped Raven off at the daycare Monday morning and then headed to the office. The whole way, she couldn't stop thinking about the way Tyson had touched her hand Sunday night as they walked to her car, brushing against her skin as gently as if she were a delicate butterfly and he was afraid of brushing off the colorful scales.

Not that their last kiss had been delicate. Every nerve in Amber's body had awakened to Tyson's nearness, and her head had started screaming out a red alert warning.

She shook off thoughts of Tyson and stepped into Violet's office.

"How did Sunday's wedding go?" she asked.

"Without a hitch," Violet said. "Ava got rave reviews. How about yours?"

Amber felt a stab of jealousy. It wouldn't be easy to get this promotion if they both performed well. She considered covering up the crane fiasco but decided to go for honesty. "Not exactly hitch-less. The sprinklers went off in the dining room before the wedding, and it was a bit of a scramble to replenish the supplies and clean it up. I think we took care of it." She cocked her head, suddenly worried. "Did the bride complain?"

Violet shook her head. "I had no idea there was a fiasco. She loved the wedding. In her mind, everything went perfectly. So whatever you did to fix it, it worked."

Tyson fixed it. Tyson had saved the wedding. Amber released a quiet sigh of relief and nodded. "The venue really pulled through. They got it all cleaned up so it looked like nothing happened."

"Yet another recommendation for the Crescent Hotel. Speaking of which, I know it's not your favorite venue, but we've got two more bookings for next month at the Crescent. Do you want to take them?"

"I think the hotel is growing on me. I don't mind working there so much anymore."

"Perfect. You can have them both."

"And Ava?"

"She's got others she'll be working on. But we've got two weddings before we even hit the weekend, and I want you at the garden wedding on Wednesday. Can you head out to the Blue Spring Heritage Center and see what it's looking like? The bride is anxious. She might meet you out there."

Amber grabbed the clipboard with the checklist off the hook. "I'll check it out and make sure it's up to par." She'd worked the Heritage Center before, though, and knew they were up to snuff. No sprinklers, either. This wedding would go smooth as ice.

♋

As expected, the Blue Heritage Center garden area was pristine and ready for a wedding. The stream behind the gazebo set the perfect backdrop for pictures. Amber snapped a few and made notes in her portfolio.

"You don't need to come up here," she told the bride on the phone as she wandered the grounds. "You can if you'd like, but I've taken several pictures. I'll send them to you."

"I think I'll come anyway," the woman said, her voice nervous on the phone. "I just have to see for myself."

"Sure, that's fine. I'll wait until you get here."

That was the plan, anyway, until Raven's daycare called.

"No," Amber groaned as soon as she saw the familiar number.

"Ms. Morris?" the worker's voice said. "Raven's running a fever again. We need you to come get her."

"I'm telling you, she's not sick!"

The argument was futile. Amber ground her teeth together in frustration and headed for her car. She left instructions with the Heritage Center to show the bride the grounds, and then she went to the daycare. Why did this keep happening to her? She blinked back angry tears. She couldn't use Clarissa during the day because Clarissa had a real job. For now Amber was on her own.

Tyson called while Amber was driving Raven home. Amber didn't answer, afraid he'd hear Raven wailing in the backseat.

It wasn't really Raven Amber was annoyed with. She took her temperature and gave her baby medicine before wrapping her in a blanket and settling onto the recliner with her.

"Poor little girl," she sighed, rocking her back and forth. "I guess it's time to get you to the doctor."

Her phone dinged as a text message came through. She smiled when she saw it was Tyson.

Want to do something tonight?

Yes. Her soul ached to see him like he was a magnet pulling

her to him. But Monday was the one day Clarissa had her class, and Amber couldn't leave. She texted back.

Would love to, but can't. Tomorrow?

I'll hold you to it.

Amber put the phone down. She hoped he would.

Tuesday found Raven with no fever and Amber back at the Heritage Center. Her thoughts flew back to Tyson every few minutes even as she tried to concentrate on supervising the wedding set up. When his name danced across her phone screen around lunchtime, she wondered if she had conjured his call.

"Hello?" she said, answering the phone.

"Hey, you don't screen my calls anymore," he said teasingly. "I've moved up in the world."

He had in her world, anyway. His voice brought a smile to her lips. "You're not some strange hotel manager following me around anymore."

"Now I'm the familiar hotel manager following you around?"

You're the hotel manager I want to kiss me again. But Amber didn't say that. "Something like that."

"I'm about to take a lunch break. Want to meet?"

Of course she did. But a quick glance around showed she couldn't leave. "I can't. We have a wedding rehearsal tonight and I'm in the middle of supervising set up."

"What if I brought lunch to you?"

Amber brushed away a bead of sweat as it dripped down her face. Good thing the wedding was in the evening, or the ninety-degree weather would roast them all. "Actually that would be lovely. Can you bring me a tall glass of lemonade also?"

"You got it. Where are you?"

"Blue Spring Heritage Center."

"Great. See you in half an hour."

He didn't ask her what she wanted, and she found herself tingling with anticipation of what he would get her. Did he know her well enough to know what she'd want?

A strong gust of wind blew in, picking up two of the pop-up tents and blowing them several yards away.

"Hey," Amber called, feeling a flash of irritation. "All of these tents need to be sandbagged down." That wasn't her job, but if a tent blew into the stream behind them, she was the one who would be in trouble.

"Sandbagged down?" A young twenty-something-year-old boy said, looking at her in confusion.

Who set up event tents and didn't know about sandbagging? "Where is your supervisor?"

The man just looked more confused, and the more she looked at him, the more Amber thought he looked like a teenager rather than a twenty-something. "He called in sick and they sent me to put up the tents and chairs. They made it sound easy."

Amber threw her arms up. "Well, it is, if you know what you're doing." Great. Now she got to be the one in charge. "Go get those tents and bring them back."

She looked around for someone else from his crew. She spotted one putting the extra folding chairs into the back of a trailer. She stepped up to him and asked, "Can you get me a bucket? You probably have some in the trailer."

"Buckets. Yes. I think we do."

Amber followed him.

Another crosswind blew through. It picked up a tent near the chairs and tossed it into a line of small trees. The tent immediately caught on the branches. The younger guy ran over and began yanking on it.

"Stop!" Amber shouted. If he yanked hard enough, he would rip it, and then they would be down a tent.

He froze his actions and looked at her.

Amber marched over to him. "That's not how you get a tent free."

"Do you cause trouble everywhere you go?"

She whirled around, all worries about the tent fading.

"I seem to," she admitted. Her eyes raked over Tyson. He wore his green work polo with the Crescent Hotel logo in the corner, paired with beige pants. He looked tidy and professional, very different from the boy in Bermuda shorts a few days ago jumping off the dock into the lake.

Somehow both looks fit him.

He put a plastic bag of to-go boxes down in one of the chairs and stepped over to the boy with the tent. "Let me help you get that down before you rip the canvas."

"Here are the buckets."

Amber would rather watch Tyson save the day, but she turned to the other man and accepted the buckets. "There are probably sandbags in there too. Did you see any?"

"I'll check."

"Amber," Tyson called, "where would you like this to be?"

He had freed the tent and held onto one leg while the boy held another. The two others dangled sideways, and Amber stepped over to grab one.

"It goes over here."

Together the three of them maneuvered the tent where it belonged. Another tent blew off with a gust of wind, and Tyson ran after it while Amber showed the boy how to tie down the buckets.

"When you put sand in here, it weights the tent so it can't blow away. Wind will always be a factor anywhere you go, so get in the habit of weighting your tent."

"Good thing you're here to explain these things," he joked.

"Good thing." In the end, after all, that was Amber's job. To make sure everything went smoothly and any unexpected hiccups were remedied.

She joined Tyson where he was setting up the other tent.

"You should know better than to let your tent flyaway," he said, giving her a little grin that let her know he was joking.

"Apparently not everyone knows you're supposed to weigh them down. Thanks for coming along."

"I'm here for anything you need." He pulled his phone out of his pocket and checked it. "But lunch break's only an hour, and it took me twenty minutes to get here, so I've got to go."

"Oh." Amber glanced toward the plastic bag with the to-go boxes, still sitting unattended in a chair. "What about lunch?"

"You go ahead. I'll catch you another time." His eyes scanned her face, landing on her lips before darting back to her eyes.

Amber felt a pull toward him as if someone had hooked a string to her spine and connected it to his body. She moistened her lips with her tongue and didn't break his gaze.

His phone ringing forced him to lower his eyes.

"And that's the hotel. Time's up." He lifted his eyes again, hesitated for a second, and then bent his head and kissed her cheek. His face flushed pink, and he gave a little nod and a wave. "See ya."

Amber touched her fingers to the spot on her face where his lips had touched her, feeling as if someone had pressed a hot match there. The quick kiss surprised and delighted her. He acted so shy around her, as if every interaction was a step out of his comfort zone, never mind that he had already kissed her. Was he for real?

Her stomach growled, reminding her that he picked out her lunch. She wandered over to investigate, picking up the Styrofoam cup and taking a long sip of the lemonade first. Perfectly refreshing. Then she opened up the top to-go box. They were two, and she realized one must be his as well. Should she eat it or save it for him?

The top one held what looks like a club sandwich in a wrap. That sounded good. What did the other one hold? She opened it to find a Caesar salad wrap.

Both were good choices. The wraps had been cut in half, so she took one of each and closed the other halves inside the box. Just in case Tyson wanted his lunch back.

TYSON

Really? A broken water pipe on the third floor? The water had spilled over from one room to another, and Tyson was right there with the emergency crew, kneeling on the carpet and drying up water while their giant machines sucked it up.

"They should just replace all the pipes at once in this old place," the plumber said.

"They should," Tyson said, though he understood why Mr. Draper didn't. The expense would be astronomical. No, it made much more sense to replace the pipes in piecemeal, every time one of them busted.

At least, it made sense to someone.

Luckily only one of the rooms had a guest in it, and she was pacified easily enough with a free spa treatment for being kicked out of her room.

"Are those your plumber pants?" Jaya asked when Tyson came downstairs and threw his wet rag into the laundry basket.

"These are my plumber pants," he said, looking down at the water-stained khakis. "They also double as my taxi pants, my garbage collector pants, my waiter pants, and my pajamas."

Jaya laughed. "Crisis averted?"

"As always." But this wasn't meant to be his life. He was

meant to do something much bigger than run a haunted hotel.

His phone buzzed just as he grabbed a wrapped salad from the fridge. His heart lifted when he saw Amber's name.

You left your lunch here.

He shot off a quick response. *Enjoy it for me.*

I can't. Too much food. I'll bring it to you tomorrow.

If you insist. Maybe she just wanted an excuse to see him.

He could work with that. In fact, he could do her one better. He still had her address in his phone; he'd swing by her house after work.

The day couldn't pass quickly enough after that. He worried he was being presumptuous again, that maybe Amber didn't want to see him. But he couldn't imagine that. There was something in the way she looked at him, like she thought he could turn water into wine or plastic into chocolate.

Chocolate. All girls liked chocolate, didn't they?

He stopped at the strip after work and bought a box of chocolate from the candy store, then made the drive over to Amber's. He found himself at an apartment complex of older buildings, with woodpecker-pecked brown siding on all sides. He parked out front. It didn't look like the nicest place to live. What would she think of living with someone else?

You've only kissed her twice, and you're already thinking of moving her in? He rolled his eyes at himself.

Her car was parked out front, so hopefully she was home. He went up the three steps leading to the ground floor apartment.

The TV blared inside, and he heard Amber's voice speaking in a singsong tone. Maybe dropping by unannounced wasn't the best idea. What if she had company? He considered turning around and leaving. But he was here already. May as well see her.

The doorbell was taped, so he knocked on the door. It took several minutes, but the noise inside abruptly went silent, and then the door cracked opened, a chain still suspended across the top.

"Tyson?" Surprise flickered across Amber's features. She looked him up and down, then closed the door. He heard the sound of the chain drawing back before she opened it again. She stepped outside and closed it behind her. "What are you doing here?"

"Well." Suddenly he felt quite lame for making this appearance. "I want my lunch back."

She blinked, and then she burst out laughing. "Really?"

"No. But it was a good excuse to see you. Plus I bought this big thing of chocolates and couldn't eat it by myself." He pulled out the plastic bag and held it out to her.

Amber accepted it, then stepped down and sat on the steps. "You didn't have to do this."

He sat down next to her. What was he supposed to say to that? Fairly obvious. "Sorry if this is a bad time. Do you have company?"

"No." She glanced at him, and he thought her cheeks colored slightly, but it was hard to tell from the street light over the parking lot. "I was on the phone. Did you apply to law school yet?"

He hadn't even pulled up his list. "No, but I will. You inspired me."

"You were already on the right path. You just needed some encouragement."

He scooted closer. "It's nice to have someone interested in encouraging me."

She lowered her eyes but smiled at him through her lashes, and that was enough encouragement. He pressed his forehead to hers, and her breath caught. He put a hand to her cheek, tilting her face slightly, then kissed her the way he'd been dying to since he'd seen her that afternoon. His hands slid down her shoulders, then to her hips.

She pulled away, shifting sideways and looking toward the street. "Tyson," she began, and he already knew what she was going to say.

"Hey, I'm good," he said, moving his hands from her hips and resting one lightly on her thigh. "We don't have to do anything you don't want to." That was why she wanted to be with him on the porch, right? To make sure they didn't take things all the way?

She was silent, then she looked at him. "For how long?"

He blinked, not sure what she meant. He sensed this conversation had somehow become serious. "How long what?"

"For how long are you good?"

He shook his head, then reached over and took her hand. "I'm still not quite sure what you mean."

She sighed. "Never mind."

She didn't take her hand away, but she didn't return his grip, letting him know he'd missed a key clue here. He pondered over her words, trying to make sense of them. "Are you asking how long I can wait for you?" he said tentatively.

She lifted a shoulder. "I guess. Something like that."

"Forever, then."

She shook her head. "No guy waits forever."

The dark tone in her voice clued him in. Ah. She meant sex. He considered those words, mulling them over. If she never wanted to sleep with him, would he still date her?

Now her words meant something. For how long?

She turned to face him. "I'm sorry. I'm asking you serious

questions. I guess what I mean to say is, I'm not gonna have sex with you. Not now. Maybe not ever."

"Okay." He nodded. "Sure."

"It's not personal. It's to protect myself. Because if I give that part of myself to someone, I expect commitment in return. And I've not met a guy willing to give it. I just want that out there, right now."

"You don't have to explain, Amber. I wasn't envisioning different ways to get into your pants."

"Really?"

"Well, maybe I had thought of one scenario," he admitted, and he felt a sense of relief when she laughed. "But honestly, Amber, you've met the wrong kinds of guys. It's your body. If you don't want to, we won't. It's that simple."

She met his eyes, the unspoken question on her face. For how long would it be that simple?

He didn't have an answer for her. He squeezed her hand. "We can still kiss, right?"

She was still giggling when she leaned over and pressed her mouth to his.

Connor and Moki texted Tyson and told him to meet them at the Rowdy Beaver. He tried to convince Amber to come, but she wouldn't, and he eventually gave up.

As he parked in front of the bar on Spring Street, he asked himself why he was there. He'd rather sit on Amber's porch all night.

He spotted Connor and Moki sitting at a table. A quick scan revealed Regina and another girl at the bar, grabbing a couple of beers. Regina laughed and joked with the bartender like they were old friend. Maybe they were.

"Hey," Tyson said.

"Hey," Moki said.

Connor nodded before taking a sip from his bottle. He slid one along the table toward Tyson. "I got a favor to ask."

"Really?" Connor didn't usually ask for favors. Tyson uncapped his bottle. "What's up?"

"My cousin's getting married. She's keeping it simple, but I thought it would be nice to hire someone to organize it. Kind of my wedding gift to her."

"So you want me to offer Amber as the wedding planner?"

"Just a day planner. Keeping it simple."

"I'll talk to her." Tyson wasn't sure how that worked, if Amber could take private clients or if she needed to work through her company. He turned to Moki. "Who's your friend? Assuming you brought the girl?"

"Just met her here, actually. Regina brought her. It's her cousin." Moki nodded toward them. "Regina looks pretty friendly with the bartender."

"Regina could carry on a conversation with a monkey," Connor said, taking another swig.

Moki turned to Connor. "You're prickly lately. Pricklier than a prickly pear."

"And you're astute."

Moki leaned toward Tyson and murmured, "I think I've been insulted."

Regina came back over, dragging the tiny red-head behind her. "Guys, this is my cousin, Elliot!"

"Sarah," the girl said, her white cheeks flushing crimson.

"You've always been Elliot," Regina said, rolling her eyes. "You can't change it now." She shoved Elliot forward. "Ask Moki to dance."

Tyson felt bad for the girl, who looked mortified. But Moki wasn't as clueless as he seemed. He pushed away from the table and took her hand.

"Come on. Let's dance."

The bartender called Regina's name, and she swiveled. "My order's up!"

Tyson faced Connor. "What's with you?"

Connor rolled his eyes. "Nothing. I'm just ready for something more."

"More than?" Tyson prompted.

Connor spread his hands. "More than this. More than my mom's store. More than—" He cut himself off and shook his head.

"More than Regina." Tyson gave him a knowing look.

"Yeah. I don't know whether I should try to revive the flame or let it die."

"Wish I could help you. I don't know either."

Connor snorted. "Like you're aware of anything other than your princess."

"Be kind," Tyson warned.

"I am being kind. She adores you. It's like she thinks you're some prince charming that swooped out of nowhere to rescue her."

"Well, I'm no prince charming—" Tyson began

"We know that," Connor said. "I don't think she does."

Regina returned to the table, her blond hair half up and falling in scattered waves around her face. She placed a glass of bubbly pink liquid on the table and grabbed Connor's hand. "Let's dance."

"Not tonight. I've been on my feet all day."

"Please?" Regina stuck her lower lip out and widened her big blue eyes, giving the puppy dog face that Tyson knew Connor would not be able to refuse.

"Fine." He put his bottle down and allowed her to haul him

to an empty space in the bar.

Tyson sat behind the table and watched his friends dancing, feeling like the odd man out. He sipped his beer, then set it down and pushed out from the table. He had better things to do than sit here. Namely, apply to law school.

Chapter Ten

AMBER

Amber woke early Thursday morning because she had a meeting with a prospective client. While she always called it interviewing the couple, she knew in reality they were interviewing her, checking to see if she would fulfill their needs and give them the dream wedding they were hoping for.

She dressed and did her hair before waking Raven. Getting Raven ready to go to daycare only took half an hour, as opposed to the hour and a half it took Amber to get ready.

But the moment she picked the little girl out of her bed, she knew something was wrong. She pressed the back of her hand to Raven's forehead, but she didn't need a thermometer to know she was running a fever.

"No," Amber moaned. What would she do now? She couldn't take Raven to the daycare; they would just call Amber and tell her to come get her. But was Raven really sick?

Raven opened her eyes and smiled at her mother. "Mama." She snuggled in closer, not acting sick at all.

"Are you hungry, sweet pea?" Amber changed Raven out of

her nighttime diaper.

"Yes. Nana?"

"Please," Amber prompted, tugging a T-shirt over the little girl's head.

"Pease," Raven echoed.

She didn't act sick. Maybe Amber was imagining the fever. She picked Raven up and carried her to the kitchen, then sat her in the high chair while she got a bowl of cereal with a banana.

"I'm just gonna take your temperature real quick, sweet pea," Amber said, grabbing a thermometer and plunging it into Raven's mouth. It only took a moment to register the fever, which was good, because Raven lasted about that long before she started fidgeting.

A hundred degrees. It was very low grade, but enough to get her sent home.

Amber leaned against the counter and put her head in her hands, pushing her glasses back up her nose when they tried to fall down.

She could give her baby Tylenol. It would mask the fever for an hour or two. Maybe the fever would be gone by the time it wore off.

"Mama, eat!" Raven ordered.

Amber sighed and wiped Raven's nose. Other than a runny nose, nothing else appeared to be wrong. She should have already taken Raven the doctor. If she had, maybe she would answers by now. This couldn't wait anymore. She'd make an appointment while Raven still had a fever.

But what about her client? She was supposed to meet with the groom in three hours. She could tell Violet her dilemma. Violet would understand. Violet would also send Ava to meet with the groom, and then she would be the face of the wedding planning, not Amber.

What Amber needed was an assistant. Somebody who did not have their own ambitions to be in charge or get a promotion.

Amber shook her head. She would just have to reschedule with the groom. First she'd make this doctor appointment for Raven, then she would call the groom and see about meeting in the afternoon. With any luck, Raven's fever would be gone by lunch time, and Amber could take her to daycare.

The doctor had an opening at ten, the same time as Amber's client appointment. Amber took it.

She held out hope that the fever would drop, checking every ten minutes.

I'll give myself until eight-thirty, Amber thought. *If the fever hasn't broken by eight-thirty, I'll call the groom to reschedule.*

It didn't break. Raven pushed her popcorn machine around the room, talking to herself in her high-pitched voice. Her heart in her throat, Amber stepped outside to call the groom.

"Hi, Clyde," Amber said when he answered. "This is Amber Morris, the wedding planner. How's it going?"

"Good, good," he said, and the rushing noise that accompanied his words indicated he spoke from inside a moving vehicle. "We're meeting at the trolley station, right?"

"That's right," Amber said. "I've had a little bit of a hangup, though, and one of my appointments has gone longer than expected." Like, all morning. "I was wondering if there is a possibility we could reschedule for tomorrow?"

The silence that hung on the line brought a sinking feeling to Amber's heart. When his voice came back, he didn't sound as congenial as he had only moments before.

"I had to take off work to come this morning. I'm driving in the way from Fort Smith. It's an hour and a half away, and I have to be back by one. I can't just pick up and do this another time. Are we gonna be able to make this work or not?"

Smokes. Amber closed her eyes. She should've called him this morning when she wasn't sure. She had no choice now. Either she found a way to do this, or she had to turn the job over to Ava. "Oh no, we can make this work," she said, inserting false cheer into her voice. "I can't be there this morning, but I'll send my assistant to meet with you. We'll get everything sorted just perfectly. Thank you so much for taking time out of your day to come up here."

"I'm happy to," he said, and his voice was amenable again. "This is what my fiancé wants, and I'll do anything to make her happy."

There it was again, that little stab of jealousy. Such devotion, such care. Amber wondered what it would be like to be so cherished. Drake had never even seen his baby girl. He sent her a birthday card when she turned one, but by the time she turned two, he seemed to have forgotten.

"Fantastic," Amber said, asserting herself back into the present. "I'll give you a name and a description as soon as I know which of my associates will be meeting with you."

"Thanks. I look forward to hearing from you."

Amber hung up the phone and sighed. She drummed her fingers on the counter, not anxious to admit defeat and ask Ava to meet him for her.

An idea came to her so quickly that she immediately dismissed it. No. She could not ask Tyson for help.

She would have to ask Ava.

Her sense of pride and independence wilted. If she could pull this off without asking for Ava's help . . .

Tyson has a job, she reminded herself.

But he said he would help her with anything she needed . . .

Just ask him! If he couldn't do it, he would say no, no harm done. Well, except maybe a little bit of wounded pride that she had to admit needing help.

But if she had to give this job to Ava, her pride would be wounded far more.

She made up her mind and dialed Tyson's number.

TYSON

Tyson parked his car in front of the trolley station and took a deep breath, then let it out slowly. He'd agreed to do this only because Amber was sick, and how could he leave her hanging? But he already regretted it. The guy would know for sure that Tyson was a fraud.

He spotted a man just a few years older than him, sitting on a bench and consulting his phone.

"Get out there, Ty," he murmured. If he didn't, the man might call Amber and complain, or worse, call her boss. He grabbed up the clipboard with the questions Amber had given him and got out of the car, closing the door gently behind him.

"Are you Clyde?" Tyson asked, stepping up to the bench.

The man looked up. "Hi, yes. You must be Tyson from Tying the Knot?"

"Yes, I am. I'm helping Amber out today."

"Good. I got worried for a minute there that this company wasn't as professional as they seemed. She sounded willing to back out of our appointment. I can't work with people I can't rely on."

Tyson straightened his shoulders, fighting back the urge to rush to Amber's defense. "Oh, these people are great. Amber's the best you'll ever find."

Clint eyed him. "These people?"

Tyson cursed his slip of the tongue. "The wedding crew. I'm just an assistant." He gave his best managerial smile. "If you're ready, we can go over these questions now."

"Go on."

Tyson read from his phone and cleared his throat. "So what's your budget?"

"We're hoping to keep it under one grand."

"Under one—are you—" *crazy?* Tyson choked back the word. He knew how much weddings were at the Crescent, but maybe elsewhere they ran less. "Sure? I mean, sure. We work with all kinds." Yep. All kinds of crazies. He read the next question. "How many people are you inviting?"

"About a hundred, between the two of us."

Tyson lowered his phone and stared at the guy. "Are you planning to feed them all peanut butter and jelly?"

Clyde furrowed his brow. "Of course not. We'll have a caterer. My fiance's mom."

"Ah." Okay. So that could help drive down the costs. Next question. "What's your dream venue?"

Now Clyde sighed. "Veronica would really like to use the Melonlight Ballroom, but it's way out of our price range."

Way out. Tyson nodded.

"So we were hoping your company would know of a place similar but for less." Now Clyde looked at Tyson expectantly.

And, of course, Tyson had nothing. "Yeah, sure. We know of lots. We'll make a list of options to share with you." Sweat beaded on his forehead, a reminder that early August in Arkansas could be even hotter than July. "Let's move this indoors and we'll finish up the questions."

Then Tyson could high-tail it out of here and let Amber handle the shoe-string budget guy with high expectations.

Chapter Eleven

AMBER

A mber tried not to think about Tyson meeting with her client. He had this. He could do it.

"Let's get this over with," she said as she buckled Raven into the five-point harness in the back of the car. "I can't keep missing work for some phantom illness. I need answers."

"Hi, Mama," Raven said, her hands distracted by the stuffed animal in her lap.

"Good girl." Amber patted Raven's cheek and closed the car door.

She hadn't notified the daycare this morning that Raven had a fever. With any luck, by noon Raven would be at daycare and Amber would be at work. Everything would be right with the world.

Her phone dinged as she signed the privacy agreement form at the clinic. Amber glanced at it quickly. Tyson. Her stomach clenched. Had something gone wrong already? She grabbed the phone and swiped it.

Don't worry about the client. Went great. Call you later. Feel better.

A warmth filled her chest, and Amber gripped the pen a little tighter as she signed her name. This boy was having an effect on her. How could that one little message have such an impact?

Of course, she'd had to lie to get his help. He thought Amber was sick, since he didn't know Raven existed. Was it time to tell him about her? Why wasn't there a guide book to follow?

Amber settled Raven down in the waiting room just as a nurse's head poked out of the glass door and called, "Raven Morris?"

Amber stood right back up, lifting Raven and balancing her on her right hip.

"Hi," the pretty young nurse said as she ushered them into the hallway. Her thick black curls were held back with a green headband, the perfect compliment to her ebony skin. She glanced down at her clipboard. "I'm Dr. Dahler's nurse, Caroline." She smiled down at Raven. "I'm going to sit you right here and weigh you, okay?"

Raven nodded, and the nurse set her on the scale.

"Oh, you did so good!" The nurse said, and Raven gave her a toothy grin. The nurse lifted her face to Amber's. "Let's get you back to a room and you can tell me her symptoms while I take some vitals."

Amber nodded, put at ease by the nurse's bedside manner.

"All right, little pumpkin," the nurse said when they entered the examination room. She laid Raven back on the examining table and drew lines on the paper to indicate Raven's height, then sat her up and took her temperature and blood pressure before looking at Amber. "Why are we seeing her today? What seems to be the matter?"

"Well, I don't really know." Amber waved her hand in a

helpless circle. "She keeps getting this fever. It's really low grade, and I can't figure out anything that could be wrong. But it's been happening several times a week, and every time it does, the daycare calls. I have to miss work, and then everything is a mess."

The nurse nodded, bobbing her head as she typed into the computer. "Any other symptoms? How is she eating?"

"Fine. She's eating fine. She's sleeping. Sometimes she gets a runny nose, but that's all I can tell."

"Okay." The nurse gave another charming smile. "The doctor will be in to see you shortly."

Amber looked around the little room while she waited. She sat in a hard plastic chair, and a book rack was nailed into the wall beside her with several children's books. Raven spotted them at the same time.

"Book, Mama?" she said.

"Sure." Amber sidled over to the examining table beside Raven and began to read to her.

The door opened, and a tall man with short cropped blond hair and wire-framed glasses walked in. He offered his hand.

"Hi, I'm Dr. Dahler." His eyes went from Amber to Raven. "And you must be Raven."

She averted her eyes in a sudden bout of shyness.

Turning back to Amber, he said, "What seems to be the problem?"

Amber sighed. "Well, like I told the nurse, she gets these random fevers. They're not that high, but the daycare calls me every time it happens. I have to go get her, it takes a day off work, and I just want to make sure there's not some underlying problem." She tacked on the last sentence so the doctor wouldn't think the only reason she brought Raven in was because of the inconvenience to her schedule.

"How often does this happen?"

"I'm not sure. Maybe once or twice a week."

"Does she have any other symptoms during these episodes?"

"Sometimes her nose runs. But it's clear, not like with an infection. She eats fine, she sleeps fine, bowel movements are fine." She felt like a broken record, repeating herself. "I'm at a total loss."

"Well, let's take a look."

Amber settled back in her chair to watch as the doctor examined Raven. Raven complied to his orders, opening her mouth, sticking out her tongue, breathing in then out, and letting him poke devices into her ears.

"Well, I think I found the problem." Dr. Dahler removed the earbuds for the stethoscope from his ears.

Amber's heart did a little somersault in spite of her confidence that nothing was wrong. "What is it?"

He gave her a reassuring smile. "She's teething. Looks like she's got five new teeth popping up in there. She's spiking a low-grade fever each time one comes, and that explains the runny nose. But she's not sick, and this will pass."

The relief covered Amber like a thick blanket, taking the pressure out of her shoulders. "Oh, that's great. What do I do when it happens again?"

"Just give her some ibuprofen and take her to daycare. I'm going to write her a doctor's note saying that she's not sick, and hopefully they'll let her stay. But it looks like she only has one or two more before she's done for a year."

Teething. That was all it was. "Thank you." She turned her attention to Raven. "Let's get you off to daycare."

TYSON

Tyson called Amber as he drove to her house from the Crescent Hotel. "So I wrote down all his answers. But I gotta go over them with you in person, because some things I have to explain." He paused his car at a four-way stop and waved an old lady through the intersection. Her deep blue Corvette purred as she passed him, and he lingered at the stop sign to give it an appreciative look.

Someday he'd be old enough to have a car like that.

"You have to explain?"

"Yeah." Tyson scratched his head and focused on driving. "I know you're not feeling well, so I grabbed some chicken soup from Chick-fil-a. Have you had their soup before? It's the bomb."

"Oh, I'm okay," Amber said, and she did sound more relaxed than earlier. "I wasn't well enough to meet with a client, but I'm managing myself. I made some food already. You don't need to bring me anything. I'm just about to go to bed."

He had the worst timing. "Save it for tomorrow, then. I'm almost at your house."

"You are? Tyson." She groaned. "Let me get dressed. I'll meet you outside."

She was already seated at the porch when he arrived, and she looked cozy and comfortable in pajama pants and a tank top.

"Hi." He greeted her with a kiss to the forehead, then placed the chicken soup beside her. "I guess if you're not feeling sick you don't want soup . . . it's like a hundred degrees out here."

"It is hot," she agreed. "But the soup was sweet of you. I'll have it later."

She still didn't invite him in. He suppressed a sigh. How long before she trusted him and his intentions? He pulled out his phone and opened the notes. "I hope I didn't totally botch this for you."

"How could you do that?"

"Well." Tyson hesitated. "The guy was kind of . . . unaware. So . . . I have to explain some of my answers."

Amber arched an eyebrow. "Just send them to me and we'll go over it."

Right. Tyson winced as he sent the notes to her phone. Amber's phone dinged, and she read through them, her brow creasing deeper with each line.

"Wait. His budget is less than a thousand dollars . . . but he wants a Melonlight Ballroom wedding?"

Tyson nodded. "I suggested we could do peanut butter and jelly sandwiches for his one hundred guests—"

"You did what?" Amber interrupted.

Tyson ignored her. "But he said it wouldn't be necessary because his future mother-in-law will be the caterer."

Amber gaped at him, her mouth opening and closing. "What?"

"And I told him that wouldn't be a problem." Tyson gave her a bright smile. "But I have his number if you want to call him back and tell him your assistant is an idiot and it won't work out."

Amber stared at him a moment longer, and then she burst out laughing. "I don't think I'll ask you to be my assistant again."

"I think that's wise," Tyson agreed.

"In all fairness, you went in blind, with no experience, and did exactly what I asked." She took his hand. "I really appreciate that."

He squeezed her fingers. "The next time something breaks at the hotel, I'll tell them to call you." He leaned toward her, hesitant, and was pleased when Amber tilted her face up to meet him halfway. His nose grazed her cheek, nuzzling her, before his lips landed on hers.

Her mouth yielded to the pressure. Tyson's stomach tightened, and he gripped the porch step to keep his hands from touching Amber's body. Her arms went around his neck, testing his ability to control himself. Maybe she didn't want him to control himself.

Amber broke off the kiss, scooting away from him. "Sorry. I shouldn't be kissing anyone right now."

Tyson leaned back on one hand and studied her. His heart pounded out a rapid drumbeat in his chest. "I don't care if you get me sick. Whatever you've got, I want it."

She laughed. "You don't want what I've got." Something like distress, or pain, passed over her features, and her mouth did a slight downward curve as if she might cry.

Surely this wasn't his fault. "What's wrong?"

She blinked, and the emotion was gone. "Nothing. It's nothing." She closed the distance between them and rested her head on his shoulder. "Did you really suggest peanut butter and jelly sandwiches?"

"Yes."

She slapped his arm, laughing, and then squeezed his bicep, keeping her hand there. "I wish I could have seen that."

Tyson grinned. "Maybe next time. Hey, before I forget, Connor wants to hire you to be the day planner for his cousin's wedding."

"His cousin?"

"Yeah, Lilly. She just moved here. She's technically a second-cousin, but we don't really keep track here in the Ozarks."

"When's the wedding?"

"Uh . . ." Tyson scratched his head. "I don't know. You'll have to ask Connor."

"I can't take personal clients right now, but I could do it as a favor."

"No." Tyson shook his head, feeling the softness of her hair beneath his chin. "That's not fair. Do it for pay or don't do it."

"Who's setting up the reception?"

Again, Tyson had no idea. "Somebody?"

She giggled, a lovely, velvety sound. "Maybe I can be on hand as a consultant. Just as a friend."

"And maybe Connor can tip you. Just as a friend."

"Maybe."

Chapter Twelve

AMBER

N
o wonder Connor had asked for Amber's help. Lilly's wedding was just shy of a shotgun wedding, and Amber was happy to put the finishing touches on a reception that otherwise would have looked thrown together.

Amber didn't recognize anyone except Connor. He gave her a reassuring smile as she fluttered about the dining room, doing her best to transform it into a reception hall. She stayed in the background of the outdoor wedding, hiding under the deck and feeling like an intruder. Amber's eyes widened when the music started, and instead of a wedding march to escort the bride down the grass aisle, rousing Latin salsa music spilled across the lawn. Amber rose with the rest of the guests and caught her first glimpse of the woman who was helping Mr. Connor put together the wedding that would make or break Amber's career. Though short, her long legs and sashaying dark hair gave her the appearance of height and elegance. She wore an old-fashioned white dress covered with pink roses, and Amber admired her courage. On some it would look silly, but on Lilly it looked classy.

Suddenly Amber couldn't wait to pull her aside and talk to her about the flowers for the wedding. Mr. Connor had been great, but clearly Lilly was the brains behind the ideas.

Lilly beamed at her fiance where he stood waiting for her under an arch Amber had borrowed from the Crescent Hotel, since she was doing this as a favor and had no budget. Lilly's feet danced their way across the grass, and Amber half expected her to kick her shoes off and leap into his arms.

She didn't, and when the music stopped, the ceremony continued traditionally. Amber sighed wistfully and cheered when they kissed.

Lilly didn't even change her dress before everyone moved from the lawn into the dining room. Amber made sure the napkins and plates didn't run out and waited until after the cake was cut before finding the opportunity to corner Lilly.

"Lilly, congratulations." Amber approached from the left, and the woman turned with a bright glow in her eyes.

"Thank you!" Lilly took Amber's hands. "Are you one of Nate's friends?"

"Your great-uncle's, actually. I'm the wedding planner. You've been helping me with a wedding."

"Oh!" Lilly didn't hold back but wrapped Amber in a hug. "Thank you so much for coming! And this!" Lilly gestured at the table settings and the vintage decorations. "Connor told me you did all of this! It's so much more than I expected!"

Amber felt herself warming to Lilly and her infectious liveliness. "I was happy to help. I was hoping I could accompany you to one of the greenhouses sometime in the next few weeks and see what you have in mind for the wedding?"

"Of course." Lilly rolled her eyes. "Brandon was so worried

about overwhelming me, but he should have just asked me to work with you. It will be a lot easier than being a go-between."

"Brandon? Oh—Mr. Connor." Amber nodded. "I can't wait to see what you can do."

"Once I get my feet on the ground, I hope to be more useful. I'd love to establish a working relationship with you."

Amber smiled. "That sounds like a great plan."

Amber glanced at her phone Sunday morning, making sure she had the time right. Just after ten in the morning. This was when she and Tyson had agreed to meet, wasn't it? So where was he? She'd already knocked and rung the doorbell. She pulled up his number, about to call him, when the door opened, and she forgot anything she was going to say.

He stood there, freshly showered, the clean, steamy smell still rolling off him. His hair glistened in separate, wet pieces, slightly curly and dark. And the turquoise polo he wore brought out the green in his blue eyes.

"Hi," he greeted. "Sorry, I was just getting dressed."

Which was fairly obvious. The temptation to kiss him was too much, and Amber stepped forward, planting her lips quickly on his.

He quirked a smile. "Thanks." His hands went to her waist, pulling her closer. "I wasn't quite ready for that. Let's try again."

She let him kiss her, his mouth slowly luxuriating over hers, the pressure building beneath her ribcage. Then she took a step back. "I don't know if I dare come in, after that."

"I won't let you distract me." His eyes glinted mischievously. "We've got work to do."

"Right." She followed him inside, noting the shoes scattered on the floor and the towel strewn across the couch. "You shouldn't have cleaned up for me."

He kicked the shoes into a closet and laughed. "Wait till you see the kitchen."

She followed him into the narrow corner kitchen, and her eyes immediately tracked to the sink. She nodded her approval when she didn't see a single dish, unlike when she'd come over after the lake party a few weeks ago. "Nice."

He sat at a small round table and opened his laptop. "Okay. Where should we start?"

She settled down next to him and pulled her own computer from her bag. "What have you already done?"

Tyson popped his fingers, nervous energy rolling off him. "Not much. I looked at a couple of schools. But they're all so expensive, it's a little overwhelming."

"That's okay. You pick the ones you're interested in. We can get grants, loans."

"And they're far away.

"Traveling's not a bad thing. It's just for a few years, anyway."

He shot her a sideways glance but didn't say anything. "I have a spreadsheet here of different schools."

Amber opened her computer and pulled up her own list. She'd looked a few things up after Tyson called her the night before and asked for her help. "I did some research also. Now, the thing is, every law school is going to require you to take the LSAT. It's like the ACT—"

"I've already taken it."

Amber paused mid-speech, wondering why she was surprised. "Oh."

He grinned at her, one hand tugging at his hair. "I have looked into this quite seriously for several years, you know."

"That's great. What was your score? That can help you narrow down the schools. And when did you take it?" Hopefully recently. She didn't know how long the score would be good for.

"I took it last October. So almost a year ago. I got a one-sixty-two."

"Really? That's fantastic." Amber knew from her research that his score was above average.

"Good enough to get a scholarship?"

"Maybe, depending where you want to go. Good enough to get in to most schools, anyway."

"I want to go somewhere nearby."

Amber hesitated before putting anything into her search bar. "Don't limit yourself, Tyson. There are some great schools out there."

"Yeah, but I'm not looking to be the best in the business. It could be an online school, even."

"That's not a horrible option." Amber looked at him over her computer. She sensed his reluctance to leave Eureka, but she didn't want to analyze why. "But even if you go somewhere else, school won't last forever."

He met her eyes, then shrugged and looked at his screen. "I guess it doesn't hurt to apply."

"Yes." She warmed to the subject. "You can always say no."

"And then I can show my mom I'm good enough to go to one of the elite schools, even if I decide not to." He gave a half smile. "Okay. Let's do this."

Tyson was easily distracted. Over the next hour, they narrowed the schools down to the ten that Tyson was seriously interested in. But then he wanted to turn on the TV and check sports scores, and after that he wanted to make out, then eat lunch, then make out some more.

"Tyson," Amber said, trying to rein him in after several kisses. "You're putting this off. Most of these schools start accepting people in October, and you want your application to be one of the first ones they see."

"You're right," he said, looking only mildly penitent. "But this is the easy part. The rest of the applications is the hard stuff. Like the essays. What am I supposed to write?"

"I don't know. Follow the prompts. Dig deep. Tell them the truth about why you want to go."

"To prove to my old woman that I'm not a failure?" Tyson snorted and rolled his eyes. "Yeah, they'll let me in for sure."

"You know that's not it." She lowered her voice and placed a hand on his. "You're following your own dreams. You've been sitting in self-doubt for so long that you haven't let yourself believe. This isn't about your mother. It's about you seizing control and defining yourself without being shackled by her doubts."

He looked at her, and then he kissed her again. His hand tangled in her hair, his thumb caressing her cheek. He paused, his forehead touching hers. "Where've you been all my life?"

Something tumbled in Amber's heart. She'd felt for a few days that he was falling for her, but it wasn't until that moment that she realized she was falling for him.

Smokes. She couldn't. She couldn't give into the magnetic pull he had on her heart. She already had a family, and there wasn't room for one more.

His phone rang, and he turned away, giving her a chance to breathe.

"Hey, Moki," Tyson said, and Amber sat still, listening to the tumultuous beating of her heart. "Tonight? Amber's here. Let me ask." He lowered the phone and said, "Moki wants the gang to go out tonight."

"Sure." She nodded, blinking past the rush of emotions behind her eyes. "You can go."

"I'm not going without you." He gave her a slow smile, as if she were dense. "There's nothing there for me if you're not there."

"Oh. I'll have to see." Could Clarissa cover for her? Her pulse clattered in her neck. She wasn't a free single woman. She was tethered.

He turned back to the phone. "I'll let you know. Yeah? Okay, I'll tell her." He put his phone away and looked at her. "Moki said to tell you he's bringing a girl, so you won't be alone. He's inviting Connor and Regina also."

"Great." He thought she was reluctant to be the only girl. "I just have to check with my friend. I thought maybe we would do something tonight."

"Oh. Well, I don't want you to have to cancel your plans." His eyes said otherwise.

"Let me just text her and find out." Amber stood up and went into the kitchen, where she typed out a quick message to Clarissa. *Can you watch Raven again tonight? Might be late. I'll pay you extra.* Extra. Like she just had extra floating around.

The response came back immediately. *Does this involve your man??*

Amber had to smile as she typed out, *Yes.*

Sure! You have to tell me about it.

Amber let out a sigh. *I owe you.*

Whatevs.

She returned to the table. "Okay, I'm good to go tonight. I need to get a few things done for work tomorrow, then I'll be ready."

"Great! I'll tell the guys. Pick you up at seven?"

Seven was early. "Is that what time everyone else is going?"

"No. I thought we could grab some dinner first."

"You've been buying all my meals lately."

"What can I say? I like your company."

"Dinner sounds great." Her mind raced, mulling over the complexity of having to introduce Tyson to Raven and Clarissa. "But you don't have to pick me up. I'll come there."

"That's not how a date works, Amber. The guy gets to pick up the girl. It's, like, fun."

"Well, maybe it's fun for me to pick you up."

He raised an eyebrow. "You're going to pick me up?"

"No." She floundered, her face warming. "I'll drive over here and ride with you."

"Why?"

She couldn't come up with a good reason. "Why is it such a big deal?" The words came out sounding more exasperated than she wanted. "What does it matter if you pick me up or if I meet you here? Aren't we going to the same place?" Her face flushed hot as she realized how defensive she sounded, and she immediately backpedaled. "I'm sorry. I didn't mean it to come out like that."

He shrugged. "I don't care. We can leave from my house."

Smokes. Amber closed her eyes. She'd made it awkward. She'd managed to take something simple and make him wonder why.

There wasn't anything to say now without making it seem even more important. So she just shook her head. "That's okay, right? I mean, if you still want me to come."

He laughed. "Of course I do. You think you could make me change my mind just because you didn't use your sweetest voice with me?" He smirked. "I'm a little tougher than that. I'll see you back here at seven."

"See you then," Amber said.

She walked to her car with a myriad of conflicting thoughts in her head. Tyson's affection felt unconditional. Was it? Could it stretch enough to include someone else's child?

She was afraid to find out.

TYSON

An hour later, Tyson found himself with Moki at Connor's mom's store, trying to convince him to go to the Rowdy Beaver with them.

"Why?" Connor said. "We always go there. I'm tired of that place."

Tyson didn't have a good answer. He looked at Moki.

"Because it's homey. It's like comfort food, man."

"Yeah." Tyson nodded.

Connor glared at them both.

The back door opened, and Ms. Thompson walked in. "Hello, boys!" she said cheerfully.

"Your mom's here," Moki said, practically tackling Connor. "Let's walk to the candy shop."

"Fine." Connor sighed loudly as Moki manhandled him out the door. "Be back in fifteen, Mom!"

"I'll hold it down for you, sweetie, no worries!"

Connor seemed slightly more amenable after Tyson and Moki plied him with soda and licorice, but he still wasn't committed.

"I have to get back to the store," he said after a few minutes. "I'll think on it."

"It's your mom's store. Let her handle it," Moki said.

"It's my night to close, and she's been funny lately." Connor rolled his eyes. "She thinks she's a school girl again around Dave."

"Think on it, then." Tyson handed him another package of licorice, and the three started up the hill toward the shop.

"Hey." Moki bobbed his head at two girls who walked the opposite direction on the sidewalk, and Connor elbowed him.

"Moki. They were like, in high school."

"I can't be picky," Moki said.

Tyson laughed. "I thought you have a date for tonight?"

"A date. Not a soul mate. I'm still looking."

"Not Tyson." Connor arched a brow at him. "He's got it figured out."

"I've got Amber," Tyson agreed, and he knew a silly grin had just plastered itself to his face. "She's helping me with law school applications."

"You're going to law school?" Moki put on a shocked expression.

"Shut up." Tyson took the bag of licorice from him and dug through it.

"It's about time." Connor reached for the licorice bag, but Tyson held it just out of reach. Not easy to do with a Pepsi in his other hand. "You've been talking about it for years."

"Watch out—!" Moki started, but the warning came too late. Connor walked smack into an obviously pregnant lady, bowling her to the ground. The woman beside her let out a cry and reached for her.

"Smooth," Moki jeered, but Connor had already bent to help her up.

"I'm so sorry," he said, pulling her to her feet. "I really should slow down going around corners."

"Or turn around," Tyson muttered, and Moki snickered.

"It's okay. I'm fine. Like I keep telling everyone, I'm not

fragile." The woman straightened up and gave Connor a reassuring smile, but her companion wasn't so easily pacified.

"You should pay more attention." Fire flashed in her light eyes, and Tyson was glad the murderous glare wasn't directed at him. "You could've hurt her."

Connor looked at her, his brow furrowing at her verbal onslaught. "You're absolutely right." He squinted, and then his expression lightened. "Luce? Is that you?"

The woman narrowed her eyes, blinking for a moment before recognition crossed her features. "Connor?"

"Whew, they know each other," Tyson murmured to Moki. "She isn't going to kill us."

"Yeah, I was worried," Moki whispered back.

The grin Connor gave her was a little too excited, and Tyson honed in on his friend's reactions.

"Yeah!" Connor said happily.

"I tutored you in English, right?"

Connor's grin abruptly turned shy, and Tyson knew he was witnessing more than a mere reunion between two schoolmates. He whispered to Moki, "You seeing what I'm seeing?"

"What?" Moki asked, looking around the street.

Her face had turned bright red. "Nice to see you again. My sister and I are going to . . . get going."

"Yeah, of course. I'm on my way back to my mom's store anyway. The one on the corner?"

"Oh."

"I work there," Connor said, as if it wasn't painfully obvious she was done with this conversation. "So do you live here now?"

Tyson stepped closer, about to do an intervention, when the woman hooked her arm through the pregnant lady's and pulled her off the sidewalk, out of their path.

"Yes. Bye, Connor."

Tyson exhaled. "Glad that's over," he muttered.

"Wait!" Connor bent and grabbed a leather bag from the sidewalk, then spun around and held it out to them like a desperate offering to the goddess of war. "You almost left this."

The girl offered him the tiniest of smiles before her face went rigid again. "Thank you."

She walked away, but Connor's eyes didn't leave her retreating backside. When he finally faced forward and headed up the hill, he walked right past his mom's shop.

"Connor." Tyson nudged him, forcing him to halt. "We're going back to your shop, right?" *Come on, man, get your head on,* he urged his friend mentally.

Moki snickered, finally catching on. "I think he got bushwhacked."

Connor glanced around, the dazed look still on his face. "Oh, yeah, sorry."

"Sure, she was pretty." Tyson led them back to the store and opened the door. No sign of Connor's mom. He deposited his soda on the glass counter top and leaned against it. "But seemed like more than that to you."

Connor scowled. He pushed Tyson away from the counter and handed his Pepsi to him. Tyson watched Connor wipe down the water ring he'd left behind as if the water offended him. "We went to high school together."

"And?" Tyson said. Moki leaned in also, the beads in his braids swinging.

Connor stopped shining the glass and bent toward them. "Okay, yeah, I had a big crush on her. What of it? I had a crush on half the girls in school. At some point or another."

So why was he avoiding Tyson's gaze? "What happened to her?"

"Beats me." Connor shrugged. "Last I heard, she dumped her boyfriend and ran off to a big city."

"And now she's back." Tyson studied Connor.

"Now she's back. So? I have a girlfriend, and we're happy."

"Sometimes," Moki said.

Tyson rolled his eyes. "The fire's gone out of that one."

Connor didn't respond. He turned around and messed with the porcelain antiques in the China cabinet, choosing to ignore Tyson and Moki.

"Oh, look at the time!" Tyson clapped Moki on the shoulder. "Closing time. We're out of here."

"What?" Connor finally turned around. "You don't want to stay and help me clean up?" He hauled another rag out from under the counter.

"Nah." Tyson grinned. "Meet us at the Rowdy Beaver tonight. Bring Regina, Amber will be there too. We'll watch the game."

"We'll see if she wants to."

"Come even if she doesn't," Tyson urged. Who knew? Maybe this girl coming around was a sign. Maybe it was time for Connor to find someone else.

True to her word, Amber showed up at Tyson's house at seven. They ate at a Casa Mexicana and moseyed along the strip hand in hand, enjoying the humid August weather. Tyson didn't even want to head to the bar, but Connor had decided not to come. Tyson needed to support Moki in his quest for a soul mate.

Moki introduced them to his date, some chick named Tasha who Tyson hadn't met before. Amber greeted her cordially, then she turned to Tyson.

"Want to dance?"

No. Never even crossed his mind. "Sure, if you do. As long as you don't mind my two left feet."

"They'll go perfectly with my two right ones."

He laughed. She always knew exactly what to say. Tyson had always mocked those who tried to turn the tiny space in the Rowdy Beaver into a dance floor, but now he found he didn't mind it at all. He gathered Amber in close and held her tight while they slow danced to the song, careful not to bump into the two other couples trying to take advantage of the floor space.

They didn't speak while they danced, and Tyson thought he could stand like that with her forever. Then the song ended and a faster-paced one came on. Tasha squealed and began carrying on her own one-man dancing show.

"Dance with me, Amber!" she said, pulling Amber away from Tyson and getting her into the dance moves. A few other girls joined Tasha and Amber, and Tyson and Moki backed their way over to the table. Amber couldn't stop giggling, though Tyson thought she looked awfully sexy in her blue jeans and tank.

"Yeah," Moki said out of nowhere. "She's got it as bad as you do. Just look at the way she looks at you."

Tyson glanced at the girls again. Amber had just turned his direction, her hands above her head while her hips gyrated to the music. She met Tyson's eyes and flashed him that smile of hers, so shy yet provocative at the same time.

"Yep," Tyson said. "She's pretty much perfect."

Chapter Thirteen

AMBER

Amber's phone woke her early on Saturday morning of Labor Day weekend. Sunlight already streamed through the window in spite of the blinds, and she lifted her head, vaguely wondering if she had slept through something.

It was Violet. And it wasn't even seven in the morning yet. Amber sat up, adrenaline pumping through her system. She had the day off, didn't she? She was in charge of tomorrow's wedding. She cleared her throat and answered the phone. "Hello?" She hoped she didn't sound like she had just woken up.

"Amber, I woke you, didn't I?" Violet said. Her voice was calm, but there was a sense of urgency in her tone.

"It's fine. I'm fine."

Violet cleared her throat. "Ava is sick. I'm driving back to town to help with the wedding, but I won't get there in time for set up. I need you to cover."

"To cover?" Amber's mind did rapid calculations. She had the day off. She was supposed to spend it with Tyson. This was part of being a team player, though. If she didn't step up to the bat now, when Ava needed her, it would look bad for her career.

Tyson would just have to understand. "How far away are you?"

"I'm just north of Little Rock. It will take me two, three hours tops to get there. The wedding is at eleven, so I should make it in time, but somebody needs to be on site doing the prep work and getting organized."

"Do you have the spec file? This is the one at Thorncrown, right?"

"Yes, and I've already emailed it to you."

Amber ran through what she knew of the wedding. "I can handle this, Violet. You don't need to come back."

"I don't want to put this on you—"

"If I'm going to be there to set up, I'm going to stay to see it through. We don't need to both be there."

Violet hesitated, then said, "You're right. Thank you, Amber. I knew I can rely on you."

Violet was just lucky Amber was in town. "Absolutely. Go enjoy your trip."

Amber hung up the phone and took a deep breath, categorizing her to-do list. Good thing she already had Clarissa scheduled to babysit until the afternoon. First, she needed to call Tyson and cancel. Then she needed to get to the Thorncrown Chapel.

Tyson answered on the second ring. "Hello?" he said, his voice gruff with sleepiness.

"Oh, I woke you, didn't I." Great. That was what Violet had said to her.

"No worries. Just tells me you're as eager to spend the day with me as I am to spend it with you."

"I am," Amber said, unable to deny the disappointment she felt. "But something's come up with work, and I'm not gonna be able to make it."

"I thought you had the day off." He didn't sound accusing, just surprised, curious.

"I did. Apparently my coworker is sick and my boss is out of town for the holiday, so . . . it's just me."

"It's just you? Where is the wedding at? Maybe I can help."

Having Tyson there would definitely liven things up. "Oh no, you don't have to do that," Amber protested.

"Just consider me one of your employees for the day. Come on. I was excited to spend the day with you."

Who was she to deny him? "All right," she said. "It's at the Thorncrown Chapel."

"What time do we have to be there?"

"I'm leaving in half an hour." Just as soon as Clarissa arrived.

"I'll see you then."

Tyson showed up at the venue just as pressed and pristine in his black suit as any of Violet's employees. He stepped over to where she stood by the piano, helping the pianist organize her music. He put a professional expression on his face and held his hand out.

"Give me a list. I'll make sure it gets done."

Amber looked at him, and somehow the no-nonsense look on his face was just as sexy as his playful one. "Oh, you're here." She turned around and rifled through her folders. "I didn't make one for you. Here." She removed the seating assignment map and handed him a plastic container of name cards. "Make sure these are all in the right places."

"You got it." He gave her a small smile, the only thing to indicate that their relationship was more than business. He turned and walked away, and Amber stared after his well-fitted pants until the pianist cleared her throat and re-directed Amber's attention.

"Yes," Amber said, remembering the matter at hand. "Let's go over the order of entry."

The wedding went off nearly flawlessly, which was all Amber could ever hope for. Tyson stayed while they cleaned up after the reception, and only after he and Amber had slammed the last bit of decorations into the trunk of her car did he gather her into his arms.

"You are so hot when you're bossing everyone around and taking charge."

Amber blushed but didn't try to escape his hold. "You're the one who's a natural out there. I would've thought you were the wedding planner."

He spun her around, shifting his hands to her hips and leaning her against the back of her car. "I know how to manage people, but there was no mistaking who was in charge out there." He pulled her ever slightly closer and dipped his face to hers, nuzzling her cheek with his nose.

Amber hummed to herself, relishing the closeness of their contact. He didn't try to kiss her, but he caressed every inch of her face with his nose and his cheek, the scruff on his face scratching her skin. She shivered and moved closer, her hands clutching his upper arms. His mouth neared hers, his breath whispering across her lips. But still he held back. She whacked his arm and laughed.

"You're teasing me."

He took a step back, shoving his hands in his suit pockets and putting a foot of space between them. He grinned at her. "Just trying to make you want me more."

It was definitely working. "Did you plan to hang out in this parking lot all afternoon, or was there something you wanted to do?" Her hand slipped down his forearm, and her fingers touched his. He took the initiative and slid his hand through hers, wrapping around her fingers in a backward grip.

"What's your curfew? There's a fireworks show at Basin Park tonight to celebrate the Mexican Independence Day. The festival's already going on. Food trucks, live music. We could go just before dark. Interested?"

The offer was tempting. She bit her lip, wondering if she could entice Clarissa to stay longer. "I have a few things to do at home. Let me see if I can make it work."

Amber was in luck. Clarissa had nothing else going on that night and agreed to come back in a few hours to sit with Raven.

"I promised my mom I'd come over and watch a show with her," Clarissa said. "So I can't come before eight. But it's a good opportunity for me to get away and study. Raven's easy to watch while she sleeps."

"Thank you so much, Clarissa," Amber said.

Clarissa waved her off. "Just don't let this guy slip through your fingers. He seems like a keeper."

"He is," Amber agreed.

She texted Tyson after putting Raven down for a nap. *I'm good for tonight. Still in?*

She didn't have to wait long for his response. *I'll pick you up at six.*

Oh no, he wasn't coming here if she could help it. She responded, *I'll be in town already. Meet you at the park at eight.*

Amber put on her favorite blue jeans and a light sweater. The days were still sweltering, but September brought a nice breeze in the evenings, especially by the springs.

At seven-thirty someone knocked on the door, and Amber opened it. Clarissa stood there.

"Hi," Amber said, ushering her inside. "Thanks for agreeing to come back and watch Raven tonight."

"No problem." Clarissa gave her a warm smile. "Don't hurry home on my account. We'll be fine."

"Thank you." Amber grabbed her purse off the hook by the door and then hurried out.

Parking by Main Street was full. Amber parked on Mountain and hiked down. She texted Tyson as she neared the park. *Here.*

I've got a spot by the red food truck. Head that direction. I'll watch for you.

Amber did as instructed, spotting the row of colorful food trucks near the street and moving toward them. Her eyes scanned the area for Tyson, and then she saw him. He stood by a blue blanket spread across the green grass, his phone in his hand and the other one moving back-and-forth in the air, his eyes on her.

A warm rush of delight flooded her chest, and she waved back.

"Hi." Amber sidled up to him, inexplicably shy. He had changed from his formal wear into a dark blue T-shirt that read "I taco for you" and jeans. Somehow the casual clothing felt even more intimate than his suit from earlier. She brushed her hand through her short hair and looked down at the grass.

"Hi." Tyson slipped a hand behind her head and kissed her forehead. "You look nice."

Her shyness melted away, and she leaned into him, inhaling the scent of aftershave and cologne. She reached up and brushed the skin on his chin, noting how the bristles from earlier were gone. "You too."

"I saved us a spot. A good one, too." Tyson grinned and gestured to the blanket on the ground.

Watching the sparkle in his eyes, Amber didn't care at all if she saw a single firework. "Sounds great."

TYSON

The sun had begun its dip on the horizon, and as the chirp of crickets grew louder and the mosquitoes buzzed nearby, the mariachi band started up a cheerful, rollicking melody.

"Soon," Tyson said, pulling Amber down to the blanket with him. "They'll start the fireworks soon."

"No Connor or Moki?"

Tyson paused, then decided this information would matter to her. "Connor and Regina broke up."

"They did?" Amber straightened enough to shoot him a wide-eyed look of surprise. "When did that happen?"

"Like, two days ago." Connor had come over in a rage, mad enough to spit nails. He finally had proof of Regina's lying ways. Too bad it only proved Connor right.

"I thought they were serious."

"They got serious fast and then it died." Tyson shrugged. "I kind of saw it coming."

"I'm sorry," Amber said, looking genuinely distressed. "Is Connor okay?"

"I think so. I think he was waiting for it also." He'd seemed a little down when Tyson talked to him earlier. Tyson had told him he'd come by after the fireworks, and he made a mental note to remember.

Amber fell silent. "Well, I'm sad for them both." She picked a piece of pineapple from the blanket and flicked it onto the grass.

Oops. The pineapple was from his taco earlier. He should have saved her one. He shrugged. "They'll both find someone better for them."

"Hmm. I guess that's what people do. They like each other until they don't."

He watched her profile in the dimming light. "Sometimes they don't stop."

"And then what?"

And then what? "Well, they stay together." Get married. Have sex. Share everything. Not always in that order. "Live happily ever after."

Her lips turned upward. "Do you always come to this show?"

"If I'm in town." He lay back on the blanket, propping himself up with one elbow. "First time for you?"

"Definitely. No Mexican Independence Day celebration in Fayetteville."

Fayetteville was close enough to be local, but Amber never talked about her family. He realized he didn't know if she had siblings, what her parents were doing, nothing. "Are your parents still there?"

"No. They retired to Colorado."

"Nice. Retiring, I mean."

"Aren't yours retired?"

Tyson rolled his eyes. "Yeah, officially. But my dad was a big shot lawyer and can't seem to let the glory days go. He's in Little Rock now with my mom, trying to feel like he's more important than he is."

Amber turned on her side, and even in the fading light he

could feel her studying him. "So you don't get along with either of your parents?"

Was that a red flag? He better not tell her about his brother, then. "We get along fine. I guess they weren't the best examples of loving parents for me."

Amber didn't say anything, and Tyson was afraid to look at her. Would he see judgment or disgust on her face? "They're good people. Maybe I'm the difficult one. They like my brother well enough." Oh, shut up, Tyson. He wasn't making this any better.

"Tyson—"

"I'm sure it's me. Always afraid to make a decision, to take a step forward with life."

"Tyson, you don't have to—"

"I think some people aren't meant to be parents. Being able to procreate doesn't make you a loving parent. And they weren't. But maybe they didn't know they'd be that way until it was too late. And maybe I'd be the same way. A disappointment. And disappointed." Why the hell was he still talking? "It's best to leave parenthood to the mentally stable."

He fell silent, and Amber didn't say anything either. A brilliant light lit the sky as if the sun had reappeared, and she turned her head toward the glow. A collective cheer rang up from the crowd, and it was his turn to study her. She kept her face tilted upward, the light reflecting off her cheeks in streaks. Almost as if she were crying.

"Amber?"

She didn't look at him, her eyes on the sky as more colorful explosions lit the park.

"I said too much, didn't I?" he said, afraid to touch her even though he wanted to pull her close. His heart hurt, ached as if it had turned itself inside out. Now she knew how messed up he was. "I screwed it all up, didn't I?"

"Tyson, just shut up." She turned and kissed him. Her mouth was forceful on his, and he tasted saltiness on her lips.

He gripped her shoulders and pushed her back. "Are you crying?"

"No. No. Stop talking."

She kissed him again, and he let her, but the pit in his stomach told him something was wrong. Something that hadn't been wrong before.

♥

By the time Tyson and Amber finished saying goodbye, it was well past eight. Tyson made sure she left the parking lot safely, then drove the short distance to Connor's mom's house. He knocked on the door, and Dave, The Boyfriend, answered.

"Connor!" Dave shouted before settling himself into a chair in front of the TV. "Your friend's here."

"Hi, friend," Connor said, coming out of the kitchen. He beckoned Tyson inside, and they both sat around the table, which was covered with to-go boxes. "I didn't really think you'd come over."

"I told you I would." Tyson used his fingers to pry up a sushi roll from the foam container in front of Connor.

"I just thought you'd be with Amber all night."

Tyson chewed on his seaweed and fish for a moment, considering how to answer. He could just shrug it off like she hadn't wanted to be together tonight. Or he could spill the truth and risk looking less than manly.

He could be himself with Connor. That was one reason he valued their friendship so much. "I'm not sleeping with her."

Connor cocked an eyebrow up. "Okay. Thanks for sharing."

Tyson flipped a grain of rice at Connor. "She doesn't want to. She says she wants to be more committed first. She'd rather just get to know me and make sure we like each other for who we are right now."

"Well, there's definitely something to be said for that. It's how everyone used to do it. Can't say the other way's worked well for me."

"How's the single life treating you?"

"Regina and I never stood a chance. We jumped into bed on the first date, and then it felt like we had to make it work even though we had almost nothing in common. Except sexual attraction."

"There is that." Tyson waved a chopstick at Connor.

"Yeah, but it's obviously not everything, is it? I think I'll follow Amber's methodology with the next person."

Connor was already thinking of moving on? Maybe that was why he wasn't as broken up about Regina. Tyson remembered Connor's high school friend, the one he'd been strangely reluctant to talk about. "And have you found that next person?" Tyson arched an eyebrow.

"Maybe. Only time will tell. I'm not sure I'll ever find the right girl."

Tyson picked up another sushi roll. "I think I have."

"I think you have also."

As long as he didn't ruin it. He couldn't shake the look on her face from his mind. Was it something he'd said? Or something he'd done?

Or was it just him that was the bad luck charm?

Chapter Fourteen

AMBER

Tyson's confession left Amber deeply troubled. It wasn't even a confession, of course. She couldn't look at it like that. But his true feelings, his true fears, had come out, and the consequences were unexpected.

She couldn't pursue this relationship. Tyson was another Drake. Another man who didn't want to be a father.

The next six days passed in a whirlwind of activity with three weddings back to back on Friday, Saturday, and Sunday. It was a good opportunity for her to break away from Tyson and try to sort through her feelings.

All it showed her was that she wanted his presence in her life.

How could this have happened to her?

She had just put Raven to bed and collapsed on top of her mattress Sunday night when he called her.

Amber had sent countless calls to voicemail with lame text messages accompanying them that said things like, "Too busy to talk. At a wedding. At another wedding. Exhausted. Call you later."

She stared at his name and knew she should ignore this one, also, but her heart yearned to hear his voice. So she answered.

"Hey," he said, his tone tentative. "I was worried you were ghosting me."

"No, no," she said, feeling guilty. "It's been a busy weekend."

"Busy week," he said.

Right. A busy week. She'd found reasons not to see him every day since Saturday. "Yes." She took her glasses off and set them on the dresser, then rubbed the bridge of her nose. "I'm exhausted."

He hesitated, then said slowly, "Does it have anything to do with what I said on Saturday?"

It had everything to do with it. But not the way he thought. She heard the fear in his voice, the vulnerability, and she couldn't be one more person to deject him in his life. "No, of course not."

"Yeah?"

He didn't believe her. He'd shared something personal, and she'd bolted. Remorse lanced through her. "Really."

He exhaled. "In that case . . . Want to come over? I rented that new comic book movie. I've even got popcorn."

The invitation was tentative, braced for rejection.

"Serious?" Amber said, putting a smile in her voice. "You have one of those fancy popcorn makers where you pour greasy butter all over the top of the popcorn?"

He responded in kind, his tone becoming more jovial. "Um, no, but I do have a microwave. It can cook the popcorn and then melt the butter to be poured over the top. All in the same microwave."

Amber laughed. She lay back on the bed and draped one hand across her stomach. "Your microwave is very talented."

"I like to think it's the operator of the microwave."

She laughed again. She'd missed him. He made her feel so free, so young. Which she was, wasn't she? Only twenty-five. Not time to write her obituary yet.

Tyson was saying something, but her eyes were closing, and she shook her head to wake herself. "I'm so sorry, Ty. I'm falling asleep. I do want to see you, though. I miss you."

The words left her mouth before she'd had a chance to consider them.

Tyson paused. "You miss me?"

"Yes. I've missed seeing you. I wish you were here." It must be the exhaustion speaking. Tears gathered in the corners of her eyes, and she fought of a wave of loneliness.

"You wish I was there?"

"I'll call you tomorrow, Tyson."

"One more reason to look forward to tomorrow."

Amber hung up the phone, letting it drop down on the pillow beside her. She rolled her face and let the tears drop into the cloth.

It seemed she had barely closed her eyes when the doorbell rang. The high-pitched chime jarred her from her sleep, and Amber jerked upright. One hand closed over her glasses and propped them on her face even as her feet hit the carpet. She had only one thought—get to the door before they rang the bell again and woke Raven. Didn't the idiot know it was taped for a reason?

She stepped on a stray Lego on the way there and cursed under her breath. Who would show up at her house in the middle of the night?

A quick glance at the clock on the stove showed it was only a little after eight. Not that late after all.

She picked up a stuffed animal from the entryway and tucked it under her arm before opening the door a crack, the chain across the top tinkling. She straightened up, her annoyance dispelling when she saw Tyson standing on the porch.

"Tyson!" She blinked several times, her joy at seeing him morphing into dismay. She inched the door almost all the way closed. "What are you doing here?"

His eyes scanned her from head to toe. "You were sleeping right now?"

"I did tell you I was tired," she said, but she added a smile so he wouldn't think she was angry. "I fell asleep."

"And I thought you meant you wanted to hang out but were too tired to go anywhere. So." He lifted his hand and shook a plastic box. "I brought the movie to you. And." He lifted his other hand and rattled a plastic bag. "I even brought the popcorn and extra butter. In case you didn't have enough."

Amber laughed and leaned her head against the door frame. She wanted to invite him in. But her house was littered with blankets and sippy cups and Legos. And Raven might wake up.

He studied her, as if knowing her internal debate. He nodded at the stuffy in her arms. "At least you sleep with a friend."

Her face warmed, and she fought the urge to throw the stuffed animal out the door.

"So. Can I come in?"

"I don't know if it's a good idea."

Her warring emotions must have shown on her face, because Tyson said, "I'll behave. I won't put any moves on, if that's what you're worried about."

That was always a concern, but it wasn't at the front of her mind right now. She glanced over her shoulder to check out the condition of her house. Just as she'd suspected.

She turned to face Tyson, ready to beg his pardon and tell him no. But there was that look in his eyes, like fake bravado, like he expected her to and was steeling himself for it. To heck with the consequences. "Okay. You can come in. But I need just a moment to clean up."

He cocked an eyebrow. "You're seriously worried about what I'm going to think? Trust me, whatever the condition, I've seen worse."

She wasn't going to debate it with him. "Just give me a second." She closed the door and locked it, just in case he thought he could come in while she cleaned. Then she went around her living room like a mad tornado, gathering up toys and puzzles and blankets into a laundry basket. She closed it into the laundry room and leaned against the door with a sigh.

What was she doing? She needed to be discouraging Tyson, not allowing him to worm his way farther into her life.

But there was no denying the way she melted when she saw him. How much she wanted him to worm his way into her heart.

Now to check on Raven.

Amber slipped into the little girl's bedroom and smoothed back the wild curls around her head. Raven stirred slightly and made a soft baby noise but didn't wake. Hopefully she wouldn't. Amber's pulse raced at the chance she was taking.

She hurried back to the front door and pulled it open. "Okay. Now you can come in."

He stepped in after her, glancing around as if expecting to find some big secret tucked away. "What happened to your stuffed bear?"

She shook her head, cheeks growing hot. "I put it to bed." In a laundry basket.

He set the movie on the back of the couch and dropped the grocery bag on the ground, then turned around and looped his arms around her waist. His mouth brushed hers lightly, then captured her lips for a longer kiss, his embrace tightening. "Are we okay?" he asked when he pulled away.

Amber tugged him back and rested her head on his chest, listening to his heart beat. "Of course. Sorry I was so busy."

He found her hand and wove his fingers through it. "Something's missing when you're not with me," he said, his voice suddenly quiet. "I don't like it."

She relished the feel of his hand on hers. Tyson kissed the side of her neck before wrapping his arms around her body and resting his head on top of hers. A warm contentment filled Amber's belly.

"I don't like it when you're not with me, either," she admitted. Which explained why she felt like crying also.

"Come on, then." He stepped away from her and moved to her entertainment system, where he set up the movie. "Let's pretend like we're an old, boring couple watching a show. With extra buttery popcorn coming up."

Amber giggled and settled into a corner of the couch with a blanket while Tyson disappeared into her kitchen with the popcorn.

TYSON

How much butter was too much?

Tyson proceeded to soak the popcorn, then give it a good toss with a metal spoon.

He wanted her to like this. He wanted her to like him.

In spite of what Amber said, his gut told him something had been amiss between them last week. She denied it, and she was acting normal, so maybe whatever it was had passed.

Or maybe she was withholding judgment until his next faux pas.

He returned to the living room, where Amber had the movie ready to go and was smoothing a blanket across the green fabric of the couch. Tyson put the popcorn on the coffee table in front of her and sank into the upholstery.

"All we need is a good bottle of wine to make this perfect." He looked at her hopefully.

Amber shook head. "I don't have any wine. But I think the evening will be perfect without it."

Tyson pulled her down onto the couch beside him, then smothered her face with kisses, his hands plastered firmly to her shoulders. "You may be right. But you better start that movie before I get too distracted to care."

Amber gave a husky laugh, shooting him a sultry expression before standing to push Play on the machine.

That look had his heart skipping a beat.

He was careful not to touch her when she sat down beside him again. She showed a lot of trust by letting him into her house, and he wasn't going to damage that. He was conscious of the heat of her pajama-clad hip pressed against his. Then the opening credits of the action flick started, and Tyson breathed a sigh of relief. He needed something fast-paced and exciting to keep his thoughts in the right place.

The movie did the trick. He lost himself in the fight scenes and special-effects—until Amber's fingers crept over his leg to rest on his inner thigh.

Instantly his brain zeroed in on her touch and proximity to him.

The movie continued, but all Tyson could think about was her hand. He shifted closer to her, sliding an arm around her waist. She moved slightly so she faced him, her hand going from his thigh to his chest, pressing against his skin through his shirt.

All right, so apparently she wasn't interested in the movie. Tyson could work with this.

She turned her face up toward his, and he met her lips eagerly. He put his other hand on her hip and tugged, ever so slightly, on her body.

He left it in her court, but Amber responded as he hoped. She moved from her spot on the couch to climb into his lap. Her hands went from his chest to his shoulders as she leaned forward, deepening the kiss.

Remember her boundaries, Tyson told himself, though he was struggling to keep his head on straight. He put both hands on her waist and told them to stay there.

Amber dipped her face to kiss him again, and again, and then she took her glasses off—she took her glasses off!

Somehow that act felt intimate enough that the blood flowed hot in Tyson's veins. His hands wandered away from her waist, finding life of their own. He dug his fingers through the hair on either side of her head, kissing her with a hungry desperation. He tried to hold onto a semblance of self-control, cognizant that she might expect him to be the one to put the brakes on.

A sound came from the room down the hall, like an animal knocking a book down on the dresser. Amber bolted away from him so quickly you would've thought she'd received an electric shock.

"You have a cat?" Tyson asked, his eyes lingering on her face, wanting to pull her back into the embrace. But she had already grabbed her glasses and was sliding off him.

"No," she said, a little breathlessly. She pressed her fingers to her mouth, her cheeks flushed. "I must've left a window open." She scooted off the couch and got to her feet, then grabbed his hand and tugged him up as well.

"You have to go." She pressed a quick kiss to his lips, taking any sting out of her words. "It's late, and you and your popcorn are trouble."

"I'm trouble!" Tyson couldn't resist pulling her in for one more hug. "You started this."

He pulled back and studied her face, making sure she wasn't really upset with him. He thought he'd demonstrated a decent amount of self-control, but maybe she expected more.

She responded with another quick kiss. "It's your fault for coming over here late at night when my defenses were down. It's your fault I like you so much."

Any worries he'd had about their relationship melted away. Things really were okay between them. "I can't help that part. I'm awesome without trying." He grinned, relieved he hadn't caused any further problems between them.

She smirked at him. She took him by the arm and pushed him out the door. "Good night."

He turned around. "Can I at least have my popcorn back?"

She just laughed and closed the door.

Tyson stood there grinning at the apartment like an idiot, feeling stupidly happy for having not gotten lucky. "Enjoy the movie!" he called after her.

AMBER

It was harder to keep Tyson away from her house now that he'd been there.

But she wasn't ready for him to meet Raven. Just the thought made her see spots and sent her breathing into a tailspin. Did he care enough about Amber to want to become an instant dad? Would he love Raven as if she were his own?

What if he did? What if Raven loved him too, and then things didn't work out?

The fear of the devastation she might cause on her young daughter left Amber with a migraine.

"I'm free this Saturday," Tyson said when she saw him at the hotel on Thursday. "We can go somewhere, spend the day together."

"I can't," Amber said, making a face. "I've got a wedding all day."

"Okay, no problem. I'll come over in the evening. We can watch a movie again."

Warmth flooded Amber's chest, and not just from the close call they'd had last weekend. She also remembered his kisses, his gentle touch, and even more, his self-restraint. She made a noise in the back of her throat. "I can't make it work this time."

His brow furrowed, a flicker of concern flashing through his eyes. "Did I do something wrong?"

"No, Tyson." She plucked at the skin on his forearm. "I just need to be well-rested. I have a big wedding on Sunday too. This is marriage season, remember?"

"Oh, I know. We're doing at least three every week here at the hotel." Still, he didn't look satisfied. "How about tonight, then?"

She should say no. But she didn't want to. "Maybe. What did you have in mind?"

He shrugged. "I don't know. A quick bite to eat, a movie? We can go back to my place and play pool. I could invite the guys over."

"How are your law school applications going?"

"Well. . ." he scratched the top of his head. "They're going. That's good, right?"

"How many have you sent out?"

"None."

"Tyson!" She swatted his shoulder. "What are you waiting on?"

"I haven't written the essays."

"All right." She took a deep breath and pressed her fingers to her temples as if fighting for patience. "I'll come over. We'll get dinner to go, and I'll help you write your essays."

His face brightened. "You'll do my essays?"

"How did you get that out of what I said? I'll help you. You do the essays."

"This is like high school all over again," he grumbled, but she knew it was all for show. "Fine. I'll pick you up?"

Amber shook her head. She needed to get that space between them again and keep him away from her house. "I'll meet you at your place. Have food."

Amber was not too surprised when she showed up and found tacos waiting for her.

"I couldn't help myself," Tyson admitted. "I was driving home and passed Taco Bell and thought, 'now that's totally lame' but then I thought, 'Casa Mexicana, that I can get behind.' So I did."

"I don't mind at all," Amber said, indulging in a carnita taco. "This is good stuff."

"I think so too." Tyson set his laptop up next to the food. "I'm ready." He took a bite out of his taco, and a huge chunk of tomato salsa fell on the keyboard.

Amber grabbed a napkin and scooped it up, then sent him a scolding look. "Eat first. And not by the electronics."

"Yes, Mom," Tyson said, looking properly abashed.

Amber paused. "Sorry. I didn't mean to act like a mom."

"I was just kidding." He grinned at her. "I think it's cute."

That was because he didn't know her alter-ego was a mom. He might not think that so cute.

They finished eating and cleaned up before Tyson opened his computer again.

"Okay," Amber said, scooting closer. "What's the hold up?"

"I just don't feel like doing it, to be honest," Tyson said. "The prompts aren't that hard."

Amber read through the first one. "'In less than three

hundred words, write about an issue from your academic or extracurricular life that is of particular interest to you.' Well, that's pretty broad."

"Yeah, that's part of the problem."

"So it doesn't have to be long." Amber read through a few other essay suggestions. "Tyson, you write this once, and it will work for nearly every school."

"Great. But what am I going to talk about, the hotel?"

"Think of something that interests you, something that excites you. Something you don't mind rambling about for paragraphs."

He gave her a crooked smile. "None of them asked me to talk about my girlfriend."

Amber blinked, keeping her eyes glued to the computer screen, even as the pleasure of his words rolled over her. She turned from the screen and found Tyson's gaze planted on her, the flecks of gold visible in his hazel eyes as they searched her face. Suddenly she didn't care about being cautious anymore, she didn't care what the future might bring, she didn't care what Tyson might think. She lowered her face to his and kissed him, the strength of her emotions settling from her lips to his. His nose brushed her cheek, and he whispered something, something that sounded suspiciously like, "I love you."

Amber pulled back, her eyes flicking over his face. "What?"

He wouldn't meet her gaze. "You have an eyelash on your cheek." He touched her skin with his finger and pulled the offending hair from her face. "See?"

Amber didn't even glance at it. "That's not what you said."

He gave her an unreadable expression. "I can't concentrate on writing an essay with you kissing me. You're too distracting, and I can't write an essay about the things I would like to do to you."

Heat rushed to her face, and his crooked smile returned. "Although that is a topic I could go on about for paragraphs."

Amber stepped back, her body warm. "Okay, then. Let's not let ourselves get distracted."

But even as she helped Tyson form his ideas into an outline, her mind kept going back to what he'd said.

If he'd only say it again, she might say it back.

TYSON

Wedding season showed no signs of slowing down as long as the weather was nice, and if Tyson wanted to be around Amber, he found himself attending more and more weddings as an unofficial assistant.

But now it was his turn. He'd been waiting for this for weeks, and he hoped Amber would be as excited as he was.

"The Corvette show?" she repeated over the phone.

"Yes." Tyson pushed the linen cart into the elevator with one hand while holding the phone to his ear with the other. "It's a huge multi-day event, Friday through Sunday. I go every year. It's so amazing. You wouldn't believe how many people own Corvettes in the area, and the things they do to them—"

Amber laughed. "Did you get your essay written?"

"As a matter fact, I did." He might have dawdled, taking more than two weeks to get the dang thing done. Which Amber knew, since she checked on his essay status every time she saw him. "In fact." Tyson drew in a careful breath, his nerves already jumping as he considered what he had done. "I even submitted two applications."

Amber squealed. "Tyson, that's great!"

"Yeah. Yeah, it is." The elevator doors closed, and he allowed himself a smile. "There are three other schools I'm going to submit to, and then I think I'll call it good." For this year. If he didn't get in, he could try again next year.

Or just give up.

"Then I think you earned the right to go admire Corvettes."

"And the right to be in your company?"

"Well, I'll see what I can do."

"Oh. Are you working this weekend?"

"Yes. But let me see if I can rearrange things."

Half an hour later Amber texted Tyson. *Can't Friday but I'm good for Saturday.*

That worked for Tyson.

Even after nearly three months of dating, Amber still didn't like him to pick her up at her house. Tyson knew this without asking and made plans for them to meet at the trolley station.

There was a slight nip to the early October air as Tyson drove up Van Buren to the parking lot on a hill where the trolley station was. He texted Amber as he walked inside to buy his ticket. *I'm here. You?*

Almost. In a minute.

I'll get your ticket. Meet you at the stop.

He bought two adult tickets for the day so he and Amber could hop on and off the trolley whenever they felt like. Her blue Civic pulled into the parking lot a moment later, and she joined him, a fringey blue sweater wrapped around her body.

"Cold?" he asked, pulling her in for a hug.

She allowed him to snuggle her for a moment before pulling back. "You didn't have to pay for me, I was almost here."

"I know. But it's no big deal." That was what guys did for their girls. Tyson suspected it was a precursor to the thought of sharing a household and everything he had becoming hers.

"Here, let me pay you back."

He stopped her hand as it dug through her purse. "Amber.

Seriously. Next time you get somewhere before me, you can buy my ticket."

She relented, her expression softening. "Okay."

Amber wasn't the type of girl to want to rely on someone else. He knew her independence meant a lot to her. But he couldn't help adding, "You have to get there before me, though."

She gave a laugh and slapped his arm, which only left him grinning. He grabbed her up again and gave her the good morning kiss he hadn't had the chance to do yet. She clung to him, probably reassured by the fact they were in a public location and they couldn't get too close.

And they were about to get on the trolley. The little red car with open windows pulled up in front of them, and Amber broke away, giving him a mischievous smile as if she had planned this all along. She went up the steps, and Tyson climbed along behind her, handing over their tickets.

"What we going to be doing today?" Amber asked as Tyson settled in beside her.

"Well, first we're going to the Owner's Choice car show. It started at nine, so—" Tyson checked his phone. "We have to hurry. It's already nine-twenty."

"Ah. I don't think we'll miss it."

"Yeah, but it gets crowded. We'll have to hurry or we might not see all the cars."

"Oh, that would be terrible."

She was mocking him. Tyson growled, "It would be."

"Is that it?"

"No. The awards show is after that, then there's a break before the Poker Run. We can't really watch the Poker Run, though." Tyson emitted a sigh of longing. "It's a trail the Corvettes race on by Turpentine Wildcat Refuge."

"You look so sad about this." Amber's lip twitched, and her eyes sparkled.

"Hey, it's really cool."

"And then?"

"After they get back is the Parade of Champions. It showcases the cars that won awards in yesterday's and today's shows. That's not until after dinner, though, so if you're not up to it, I get it."

"I think I'll be up to it."

The trolley dropped them off at the Village at Pine Mountain, and Tyson watched Amber's reaction as she took in the rows of shiny, gorgeous Corvettes. Some were red with white stripes, some black or dusty gray, others snazzy and bright with colors of yellow and turquoise. All had their hoods up, and the convertibles had their tops down.

"This way." Tyson gripped her hand and tugged her down an aisle. "I like the vintage ones." He stopped in front of a deep blue convertible, admiring the white pin striping.

"They are pretty cars," Amber admitted. "Not exactly family practical."

"I'm not a family man," Tyson said, and then he realized how callus that sounded. "Not yet, anyway. Besides, we don't always have to be practical, do we?"

"Not always," she said, her fingers trailing over the shiny exterior. "But usually."

He put his arm around her shoulders and hugged her into his side. "Just dream with me for a moment. A fast car, top down, beautiful autumn day, driving through the twisty Ozark mountains with trees full of colored leaves on either side."

"It sounds lovely."

"I can dream, right? Maybe someday." He took her face and

planted a kiss on her lips. "Right?"

"Of course." She looped her arms around his waist. "You can dream."

Dream with me, he thought. *Because I want you in that dream. I want that dream to be reality.*

"How much does a car like this cost?"

"Oh, way more than I can afford. Here, they have a sale lot." He pulled her through the crowd to a roped-off section of the parking lot.

The sun beat down on them, mild at first but with growing intensity. Amber paused to take off her sweater, revealing a tight purple T-shirt beneath. Her eyes were on the cars, so she didn't notice how Tyson kept his gaze on her body longer than he should.

"Which one would you want?" she asked.

He turned his attention back to the cars and perused as if he were an actual buyer. "This one." He stopped at a turquoise convertible, circa 1965.

"You like the flashy colors?"

"And the flashy cars." He shook his head when he saw the amount. "Seventy-five thousand. And that's not even the most expensive."

"So some day when you're a big-time lawyer, that's what I should expect you to be driving?"

She was teasing again, but Tyson tilted his head and considered the question. "Maybe." He'd be able to afford it.

"If this is what you want, make it a goal. Let it motivate you."

He turned to face her. She was his goal. Could he tell her that? "Tell you what, Amber. I'll make you a deal. If I get into law school, I'll start putting away money every month so I can buy one of these someday."

She tucked her hand into his and pulled him through the rows. "This one's pretty also." She paused in front of a maroon car.

"Yeah, but I like the turquoise."

"Is blue your favorite color?"

Turquoise reminded him of her. Her glasses were turquoise, and she favored the color in her clothing and shoes. "Yep." He studied the maroon car. Not a convertible, and the price tag was much lower at fifty-thousand. "What if I don't get into law school?"

"What if you don't? Does that mean your dreams are over? Why do you have to be a lawyer to own a Corvette?"

"They're pricey cars."

"So start saving now. It's not like you have a lot of expenses. Make it a priority."

He could do that. But what about Amber? If she was still with him in a few years, he hoped to be making more than an hourly wage.

The rest of the day passed in very near perfection. They stayed through the award ceremony, then got lunch and strolled through town for a few hours before the Parade of Champions.

"Let's stop by Connor's store. See if he's there," Tyson said as they walked up Spring Street.

"This is his store?" Amber asked as they rounded the corner at the top.

"His mom's. But he's here a lot." He pushed open the door, not at all surprised to see Connor behind the counter.

"I wondered when I'd see you," Connor said, grinning as he gripped Tyson's hand. He nodded at Amber. "He dragged you out this year, huh? He's got a crazy thing for Corvettes."

"I think I might like them also," Amber said.

"Figures." Connor shook his head.

"What's up?" Tyson asked. "Still chasing Luce?"

The smile Connor flashed was megawatt. "Yep."

"Things are going well?"

"Yep."

Tyson bumped his fist on the counter, happy for his friend. "Glad to hear it."

"Can't wait to meet her," Amber added, tucking her hands around Tyson's arm. "I've heard so much about her."

"We'll all get together for dinner at my mom's sometime," Connor said. "She's not really a Rowdy Beaver kind of girl."

"Neither was I," Amber growled, shooting a glare at Tyson.

"I corrupted you." Tyson gave her a quick kiss, and Connor snorted.

"Shut up." Tyson sent a dark look in his friend's direction, and Connor held his hands up innocently.

"Didn't say anything. Get on out of here and have fun, you two."

They left Connor's store and watched the parade, then grabbed dinner at Casa Mexicana before taking the trolley back to the parking lot.

The chill returned with the setting sun, and Amber pulled her sweater back on before resting her head on Tyson's shoulder. "That was fun. I learned more about Corvettes than I ever expected to."

"Thanks for coming." Tyson took her hand. "This was the best year yet. You should come with me next year."

She laughed, her head bouncing on his shoulder. "Sure. What's on the agenda for tomorrow?"

"You want to come tomorrow?"

"If you're going."

"Tomorrow's not too exciting. Just a bunch of Corvette

owners having breakfast. I don't usually go."

"We can put that on the bucket list for when you're a Corvette owner."

Tyson grinned, his chest warm with happiness. "I better work on a few more law school applications then."

She sat up and looked at him. "You know I encourage you for your sake, not mine. I don't care if you're a lawyer. You could be a bum on the street strumming a guitar for cash, and I wouldn't care."

"I couldn't very well support you like that."

She narrowed her eyes. "I don't need you to support me. I can support myself. Just follow your dreams and don't worry about the rest."

"So you'll support me?" he joked.

"Yes. If need be."

Chapter Sixteen

AMBER

"This wedding is going to be big. The biggest one I've ever put on." Amber's couldn't keep the excitement out of her voice as she sat on the floor in the office and unpacked a box of weddings supplies. "This is the one that will get me the promotion, Tyson. Are you still good with letting me use decorations from the Crescent?"

Tyson sat on the desk beside her, checking each item off a list on the clipboard as she placed it on the floor. "I'll bring them over before the rehearsal so you can set it all up. And we can use Connor Landscaping's truck to pick up the round tables."

"There's a wedding at the chapel the day before, so I can't put the rounds or the decorations up until the morning. Can you meet me there early?"

"Of course."

"I can hardly believe Violet gave this wedding to me."

"So why are they choosing to do it at Thorncrown Chapel? With the money they're spending, they could've booked the

White House."

"The money goes a lot farther this way." She glanced up at him, marveling again that he preferred to spend his time off in her office, helping her. "This wedding will be epic for a fraction of the cost."

"Epic," Tyson echoed. "I'm kind of a backyard-wedding person myself."

"Oh? Have you ever been married that way?" Amber flashed him a teasing smile.

"Never been married before, nope. But if I were getting married, I know who I would want to star it."

"Yourself, I hope."

It was his turn to smirk. "Naturally."

She didn't say anything else. She didn't ask about who he might want to co-star in his wedding. A part of her hoped it was herself, and another part was terrified it was.

"Oh, look at this," she said, redirecting the conversation to a reel of stiff white lace. She unrolled a few feet. "I need ten six-foot sections. Can you help me measure and cut?"

"You ask too much. I can't cut or measure. You're out of luck."

"Seriously worthless." She handed him a pair scissors. "I'll measure, you cut."

"That's probably the safest way to do this," Tyson agreed.

She shook her head and pulled out a tape measure, carefully marking off the pieces she wanted cut.

They'd returned to safe conversational territory, but Amber was intrigued by what Tyson had said. Where did he see himself in the future? She'd put a lot of stock into what he'd said weeks ago at the Independence Day festival. Maybe he hadn't meant that the way she'd taken it at all. "So after this simple backyard wedding you're planning," she said, probing.

"What kind of house do you think you'll live in?"

"I kind of picture a house like the one I'm living in. The one I grew up in. Nothing too big, but with a few bedrooms. A nice yard. A backyard would be nice, with a deck, for throwing barbecues and having company over."

"And space in the garage for your turquoise Corvette, right?"

"Yeah. Someday."

She didn't look up from the measuring and cutting, afraid he'd see her heart in her eyes. "How many people do you imagine filling up those bedrooms with?"

He fidgeted, a definite sign of nervousness. "You mean, like, guests? Our parents in their failing years?" He laughed, but it sounded a little forced.

"Or children," Amber said, her tone soft.

"I don't know. I haven't really thought about kids."

And yet his very response betrayed that he had.

She didn't speak for a moment, letting herself get caught up in the counting. Tyson cut the ribbon where she indicated. She set the piece aside and measured out another six feet across the floor. Then she stole a glance at him while she held out the portion for him to cut. "You don't want kids?"

"It's not that I don't want kids," Tyson hedged, his eyes looking away from her. "I'm just really nervous about doing it wrong. Being a good parent and not making my kids feel inadequate. I just think I have a lot to learn and figure out about myself before I'm ready to be a dad."

She didn't say anything, just measured out another piece of ribbon and gave it to him to cut. The disappointment sliced through her, and she swallowed back a painful lump. She hadn't misunderstood him, then.

Tyson shifted after the third cut in silence. "I'm pretty open to a lot of things," he said. "Having kids isn't a never thing. I just want to be cautious and discuss things before hand. Right?"

"Right," she said. Which would be perfectly reasonable, if she didn't already have a kid.

"Is that bad?" he asked cautiously.

"No, but." She furrowed her brow, focusing on the measuring tape. "What about when life just happens?"

"Well, let's hope it doesn't." He gave her a breezy smile. "I mean, I like surprises as much as the next guy, but some things I like to plan."

"Of course," she said, trying to smile like everything was fine.

Even though it definitely wasn't.

Clarissa called Amber that evening.

"Amber," she said, her voice catching, "I can't watch Raven this weekend."

Something was definitely wrong with Clarissa, but for a moment all Amber could think about was the predicament this put her in. She had weddings Saturday and Sunday, and Sunday was *the big one.* Now she'd have to find a new babysitter last minute? She shook herself and tried to think of her friend.

"Why? What's wrong?"

"My grandma had a stroke and they think she's going to die." Clarissa choked back a sob. "My mom bought me plane tickets for first thing in the morning. I'll be in California."

"Oh, Clarissa, I'm so sorry." Amber drew in a deep breath. She'd just have to find someone else. "Don't worry about us. I'll figure it out."

"You could try my roommate," Clarissa said. "She babysits

a lot. I can vouch for her."

Amber couldn't, and she hated using someone she didn't know. But she didn't have a lot of options at this point. "Okay. Sure. Send me her info."

TYSON

Tyson went through the standard routine at work, checking that everything was moving smoothly and in the right place, before taking the time to sit down at his desk and boot up his computer. He checked the accounts, verified the sales numbers, and made sure the housekeeping staff had everything they needed in inventory. He opened up the email account and sent off generic thank-you letters to the senders of the haunted picture submissions received the night before. Then he forwarded them onto Jaya, who would enjoy looking at them before deciding which ones, if any, deserved to be printed.

Only after he'd done the work-related things did he finally open up his own email, cup of coffee in hand. He took a sip and nearly spit it out when he saw an email from the University of Arkansas School of Law. A slurry of stinging ants took off marching through his veins. The subject read, "Tyson Hafford Law School Application Status Update."

Tyson sucked in a breath. His stomach clenched, and his hand trembled as he maneuvered the mouse over the email. Finally he selected it.

Welcome Tyson,

Congratulations on your admittance to Arkansas Law! A letter in the mail . . .

The rest of the email trailed into unimportant oblivion. Tyson ran a hand over his face and reread the opening line, hardly able to believe it.

He'd been accepted! He'd finally made it!

He had to tell Amber. She would be so excited. He'd tell her in person, after the wedding on Saturday. And then—he'd always envisioned the moment he'd tell his mom, how she'd be shocked and maybe even proud, but now he found he didn't even want to tell her. What did it matter what she thought? He didn't need her approval to validate his life. Maybe he would tell her, maybe he wouldn't. Her opinion didn't matter.

The thought was freeing. He felt as if someone had finally unshackled his future. He laughed out loud. His whole life had opened up to him, and he knew exactly what he wanted to do with it.

Chapter Seventeen

AMBER

"Hi." Amber opened the door and scanned the young lady in front of her from head to toe. She was dressed in jeans and a T-shirt and carried a leather bag. "You must be Deborah."

"Hi, yes." Deborah smiled pleasantly and stuck out her hand, which Amber gave a quick shake before inviting her into the house.

"So Clarissa said you babysit sometimes."

"Yeah, I love kids."

Amber leaned against the back of the couch and strapped on a pair of heels. "Okay. Let me introduce you to Raven, and then I have to go." She bit her tongue to keep from scolding the sitter for not arriving fifteen minutes earlier. When Amber had said she needed to leave the house by nine, she had expected the babysitter to show up a few minutes minutes before then. But that was her fault for assuming and not clarifying.

She clicked into the kitchen, where Raven sat in the high chair covered in mashed carrots. She lifted her chubby arm in what could've been a wave as she took in the new babysitter.

"This is Raven." Amber dipped her face close to Raven's and kissed her cheek. "You know how to clean her? I've got wet wipes and rags right here. She doesn't know you, so it'll be easier if you distract her here at the high chair until I'm gone."

Deborah nodded. "Don't worry, I'm good with kids. I've taken care of crying babies before."

"Right." Amber balanced back and forth on her heels, reluctant to leave Raven with this woman she didn't know. "You've got my number if you need anything?"

"Yes. And what time will you be back?"

"Should be in about five hours."

"Well, I'm off, then." Amber turned around and walked out the door without a backward glance. She took a deep breath and let it out slowly. Raven would be fine. She was used to being left with a babysitter.

Barely had she buckled herself into her seat when her phone rang. Some of her pre-wedding jitters vanished when she saw Tyson's name. They planned to meet at the venue, and he always calmed her nerves.

"Hi," she said, using her car's phone device to answer.

"Are you in route?"

Something in his voice made it sound like this wasn't just a good morning call, and Amber tensed.

"I just got in my car. What's up?"

"Better get here fast. There's something wrong with the catering arrangements, and they insist you're the only person who can change the order."

Amber's throat tightened. "What's wrong?"

"It's easier to explain if you can see it."

That did not sound good. Amber pushed on the gas pedal,

alternating between cursing under her breath and offering prayers for help. She even tried calling the caterer, but the young man who answered the phone spoke in a thick accent and wasn't very helpful.

Amber didn't have to pull out her notebook to know who the caterer was. The bride had specifically requested them for their ability to make Halal-appropriate food.

To make matters worse, Amber couldn't find parking at the boutique hotel. She would have to talk to a manager about this right away. The wedding was in two hours, and the guests needed a place to park. After five minutes of circling the lot, Amber pulled into a fifteen-minute loading zone. She'd just have to take care of this catering issue and then come move her car.

Amber hurried across the yard, through the marble entryway, and into the reception hall. Her eyes immediately landed on Tyson where he stood next to the bride, who wore a button up blouse and a skirt and was sobbing.

Not a good start.

All right. Damage control. Take care of the bride first, then find the caterer. Amber pushed her way through the people until she reached them, and Tyson gave her a look of immense relief that she was there. Amber shot him a smile before taking the young lady by the shoulder and pulling her to the side.

"Sweetie. Everything's going to be okay. What's wrong? What happened?"

"The caterer got confused—all of the food is Kosher, but it's not Halal. It hasn't been prepared correctly, and I promised my fiance I'd take care of it!"

Amber had no idea what the difference was, but that didn't matter. "Give me just a second, we'll get this all straightened out. It's going to be fine." She stepped away from the girl and stole a quick glance at the clock on the wall while she hurried over to the caterer. An hour and a half to the wedding. Two hours until the reception. Her heart hammered in the base of her neck. Not enough time to throw together a new meal.

The caterer stood together with two other men, all speaking in a different language. Their mannerisms and dress said they were not used to putting on a formal affair like this. Amber inserted herself between them.

"Guys, we have a very upset bride. What happened here? She says the food was not prepared as specified."

"The food is Kosher," a man with a clean-shaven face and a full head of dark hair said. "It is good."

Amber's head pounded with a threatening headache. She fished around on the table behind him until she found a clipboard with the signed contract. She flipped through the pages. "It says here she specified for food to be prepared Halal. We all signed it, including your company."

The man next to him spoke up, his English less crisp than his associates. "We prepare Kosher. Food is good for Halal. They can eat." He mimed stuffing food into his mouth.

Amber pointed her finger into the contract. "We asked for Halal. I need to talk to your manager."

The first man spoke up, holding his hands up as if to fend her off. "I'm Josue, the manager. I promise you all is well here. This is my restaurant. We come from Little Rock for this wedding, specific for them. All Kosher food is also Halal. The food is good."

"Wait. What?" Amber squinted at him as his words sank in. "Kosher is also Halal?" Why hadn't Amber bothered to research this?

His associate nodded vigorously, and Josue said, "Yes. Kosher is more strict. Anyone following Halal can eat Kosher, but no vice versa."

"Oh." Some of her adrenaline faded as she looked at the chargers and metal tins on the table. "Where is the food?"

"In the truck. It must be fresh when we serve it. But it's ready to be prepared."

"Did you tell her this?"

"We try, but she too upset to listen."

"It's my fault," his associate said. "I tell her food Kosher, she become angry. I could no explain."

"Okay. This is okay." Amber let out a deep breath, the pressure easing off her shoulders. "It's just a misunderstanding. Thank you." She turned around and returned to Tyson and the bride.

"All right, I need you to inhale with me. That's right. Now come take a seat." Amber guided the bride to a chair. Tyson hovered nearby, as if ready to run for a fire extinguisher or something. Amber searched her brain, drawing the bride's name from its depths. "Nida. You said the food needs to be Halal?"

"Yes. My fiance is a practicing Muslim. He was very specific that the food be Halal. He recommended this caterer to me, we've paid a lot of money for them, I don't know how this could happen!" Fresh tears seeped out of her dark eyes, and Amber fished a packet of tissues from her bag. "He's going to be so upset! He won't be able to eat anything!"

"Nida, honey, I need you to slow down, okay?" Amber handed her the tissues and knelt in front of her. "Now I didn't know this, so I'm assuming you didn't either. But Kosher food is all prepared to Halal standards. When he told you it was Kosher, he was trying to reassure you that it's correct."

"Really?" Nida blinked, a few more tears escaping. "But Adeel never told me . . ."

"I'm sure he didn't think of it. But he trusted the restaurant, right?" Amber pulled out her phone. "Here, let's call him and ask."

"I didn't want to call him," Nida admitted, a little tremble in her shoulders. "He's so nervous for the wedding, I didn't want to stress him out with one more thing."

"It's not a stress," Amber said. "It's news to you, but not to him. Give him a call." She held her phone out and crossed her mental fingers that she was right.

Nida took the phone and placed the call, chewing on her lower lip while it rang. A man's voice answered, sounding excited and cheerful. Nida turned her face, and Amber took a step back to allow her some privacy.

"Is everything all right?" Tyson asked softly.

Amber nodded. "Yes. Not what we feared. Crisis averted." She lifted her face and met his eyes. "Thank you so much for being here."

"Of course." His hand bumped hers, his pinkie finger looping through hers for a moment. "If I didn't want to be a lawyer, I'd happily be your assistant."

Nida held the phone out to Amber, her eyes brighter. "You were right. I got all worked up over nothing. The food is Halal."

"And it's going to be wonderful." Amber pulled Nida to her feet and rubbed her shoulders briskly. "Now you don't worry about a thing. This is your day. Let's get you ready."

Nida was all smiles by the time the makeup artist finished with her.

"You look lovely," Amber said. "Now sit tight. People will be arriving any minute."

And parking where? Amber suddenly remembered the parking situation and jumped to her feet. "I'll be right back."

She hurried to the front desk, where a girl with lots of black eyeliner and platinum blond hair worked the counter.

"Excuse me."

"Yes?" the girl asked, looking at Amber from beneath eyelashes so thick it might have been a caterpillar hanging on her eyelid.

"I'm the coordinator for the Hassen/Bangura wedding, and I noticed when I came in that there wasn't a lot of parking. Can we get a designated parking area? Maybe set up some cones as people are leaving? We have over a hundred guests coming."

"Oh, it shouldn't be like that now. There was a yoga convention going on yesterday, but it ended this morning at ten. There should be plenty of parking."

Amber turned around and looked out the double glass doors toward the parking lot. Sure enough, the space had opened up. "Well, that's good." She paused as her eyes landed on the loading/unloading zone, and her heart gave a little tumble.

Where was her car?

She turned back to the front desk. "Um, I'm sorry, but I parked my car out there a little while ago, and I don't see it now."

"Where did you park it?"

"Right there." She pointed to the spot. "Only a few minutes ago."

"In the unloading zone?"

"Yes." She tried not to panic. No one would have stolen it. But if someone had moved it, that meant they'd—

The girl gave her a sympathetic look. "That's for fifteen minutes only. If it was there longer, it would have been towed."

No. No way. They didn't tow her car. It had to be a mistake.

"I wasn't inside that long." How long had it been? The catering issue had distracted her, and then she'd wanted to care for the bride. Half an hour? An hour?

"I'm sorry. I have the number for the towing company."

A lump welled up in Amber's throat, and tears burned behind her eyes. This couldn't be happening. "I couldn't find a parking spot, and I'm the wedding planner! I needed to get inside!"

The girl looked properly distraught. "You can call us next time. We can put you in a spot or put a notice on your vehicle. I'm so sorry."

Amber turned away, wiping at her eyes angrily as the tears escaped. Great. Just great. "It's fine. I better go."

She stopped at the bathroom to check her appearance, but her eyes were large and red, even behind the turquoise frames. She washed them, which only removed her eye makeup and made her look sick. And her purse was in the reception hall.

Guests would be arriving. She couldn't think about herself right now. Trembling with emotion, Amber pulled open the bathroom door and stepped out, praying nothing more would go wrong.

Tyson had taken over, directing the photographer and seating guests as they arrived. He took one look at her and stepped away from the crowd.

"Amber. What's wrong?"

"Oh, you won't even believe it." Her hands fluttered, and she tried to smile, tried to laugh it off, but the stupid tears welled up again instead. "My car got towed."

"Your car got what?" Tyson gave her an incredulous look. "What happened?"

"I couldn't find a spot, and I was worried about the caterer, so I parked in an unloading zone. Then I forgot. I never thought they'd tow my car!" The tears rolled down her cheeks again, and she hid her face, embarrassed.

"Hey, now, it's okay." Tyson wrapped his arms around her.

Amber pulled away, shaking her head, hating that she looked weak in front of him. "It's so stupid. Stupid mistake."

"Don't worry about it. Really." He grabbed her chin and pressed a quick kiss to her mouth. "I'll give you a ride home and get your car tomorrow. I'll take care of it."

"I don't need you to fix this for me. I can do it."

"I know you can. But that doesn't mean you should have to. Let me help."

For a moment Amber warred against his offer, and then she relinquished. She wasn't losing her independence just because she allowed Tyson to help her. "We'll talk about this later." She inclined her head toward the wedding hall. The problem hadn't changed, but she felt calmer about it.

That was what Tyson did to her. Having him with her, tackling obstacles together, made her stronger. Not weaker.

She approached the rest of the wedding with confidence, and by the time the guests filed into the reception hall—which smelled amazing—Amber wasn't concerned with her car anymore. In fact, it was kind of a funny story. Almost.

The photographer was on top of her game, taking pictures of the happily married couple, who followed the more Western traditions of the wedding ceremony even though the food was prepared according to the groom's religious background. No alcohol was served, either, though that did not inhibit the guests from laughing and joking in all manner of joviality. Amber settled in the back to watch, the hard part over.

The girl from the front desk stepped into the hall, glancing around the mingling guests until her eyes fell on Amber. She stepped forward. "Are you Amber Morris?"

"That's me," Amber said, moving closer to her. Did she have an update on her car? She sensed Tyson approaching, staying nearby in case she needed him.

"There's someone here for you. She said she's been calling you but hasn't been able to get through. She's at the front desk."

"Someone here for me?" Someone who had been calling her —oh no. Amber's blood turned to ice in her veins. It could only be one person. "I'll be right out."

"What is it, Amber?" Tyson asked.

"Nothing," she said, probably too quickly. "I'll be back in a moment."

The girl left the room, and Amber stepped out of the reception hall. Surely it couldn't be—

Deborah appeared at the end of the hallway, tugging Raven along behind her. Raven's eyes landed on Amber, and her whole face lit up.

"Mommy!" she shrieked. She released Deborah's hand and raced forward.

Amber knelt and gathered her up in her arms, her body shaking. "What are you doing here?" she hissed at Deborah, one hand cupped behind the mass of Raven's curls.

"I'm sorry," Deborah said. "She had a fever, I kept trying to call you—"

"Amber?"

Tyson's voice came from the doorway, and Amber froze. She turned around, still clutching Raven in her arms, feeling as if she's been caught in a murder attempt.

TYSON

The little girl clung to Amber, and at first her dark ringlets and darker skin tone threw Tyson. But then his brain caught up with him, connecting the way she clung to Amber's neck to the one word she'd uttered when she'd seen Amber.

Mommy.

"Is this your—is this your daughter?" he stuttered, the blood running cold through his body. It couldn't be. Amber didn't have a kid.

Mommy.

Amber swallowed, her eyes becoming glossy. "Tyson, I was waiting for the right moment to tell you."

He pointed at the little girl. "How old is she?"

"Two," Amber said, her voice small.

He could only blink at her. Two. An entire little person rolled into a two-year-old body. This whole time, he'd thought she was the kind who didn't sleep around—but no, she just didn't want to sleep with *him*. Not that he'd assumed she was a virgin, but he'd admired her desire to—

And then he understood everything so clearly, it was like a light bulb turned on. "Ah," he said softly. "I get it now." It wasn't that she wanted commitment from him before having sex. She just didn't want to get pregnant again.

Because she had a kid. Amber had a daughter.

The implications were too big to take in at once. The responsibility, the consequences, the limitations. Tyson's thoughts muddied themselves in his head. He turned around to go back into the reception hall, not even sure what his next move would be but needing something to focus on.

Amber reached out a hand and grabbed his arm. "Tyson, whatever you're thinking, that's not it."

He threw her arm off. "You don't even know what I'm thinking." Amber had a kid. With another guy. Where was the guy now? A picture formed in his head, of Amber and some dude smiling together with the little girl between them. A family.

Where was Tyson supposed to fit in?

"Give me a chance to explain." Amber's eyes darted toward the wedding party, the group of giddy, stupid revelers, drunk on their union and happiness. "Let's talk."

Tyson grabbed the door to the reception hall and slammed it hard, hard enough that Amber winced. "Talk, then."

Amber turned to the teenager lingering behind her and handed over the little girl. "Please take her outside."

"No, Mommy!"

The child shrieked and reached her arms out to Amber, but Amber sidestepped her. She kept her eyes focused on Tyson while the screaming child was escorted out.

"I didn't mean for you to find out this way," Amber began, but Tyson quickly interrupted.

"Find out what? That you have a kid? That you share visitation rights with her dad and he'll always be a part of your life?"

Amber shook her head. "We have no contact. I got pregnant and he bolted. He's not interested in Raven and not in the picture."

"So how did you mean for me to find out? Did you mean for me to find out at all?"

"Yes, yes, of course! I just pictured it differently. I was going to invite you over for the two of you to meet, but then you said you weren't sure if you wanted to have kids, and I got scared."

Tyson couldn't follow her thought process. "Don't you think that would be even more reason to tell me? So I could decide if I wanted to be in this—this relationship?" He gestured between the two of them.

"I know, it was selfish of me, but I didn't want to lose you!" She reached for his arm, but he pulled it back.

"You should have told me!"

"I know. But I also, I wanted to be sure—"

"Sure of what? What were you waiting for?"

Amber's lip trembled, unshed tears in her eyes. She had better not cry. That would be so unfair.

"She's my little girl. I wasn't sure if it was safe to introduce you."

"Safe?" What the heck was she thinking? "You weren't sure it would be safe? Do you not trust me at all?"

"No, it's not that!" Amber cried. The tears spilled over, and Tyson clenched his jaw, willing himself not to give in to the desire to comfort her. "What if the two of you grew attached and then things didn't work out between us? What if she lost you just like she's lost her father? I didn't want to do that to her!"

"You didn't have to introduce us, Amber. But you could have told me."

Amber choked back a sob and wrung her hands together. "I didn't want to cause confusion. I was waiting for the right moment."

"And when would that be?" Tyson took a step closer. "When you felt like I'd proved my commitment? Or were you just afraid of getting knocked up again? They have pills for that, you know!"

She gasped at his words, a spark of fury lighting in her eyes. "Pills aren't foolproof."

"How many guys did you sleep with before you figured that out?" Tyson wasn't even sure where the words came from. He was lashing out irrationally, trying to ease some deep emotional anguish.

Her eyes grew wide and she pulled her hand back, and for a moment Tyson thought she might hit him. He wished she would. Confusion whirled around in his brain, anger and hurt and jealousy swirling into an ugly beast.

"I am not a whore," she whispered.

If Tyson knew anything about her at all, it was that she was not a whore. But maybe he didn't know anything about her after all. "So you say." Forget the wedding. He couldn't stay here. He turned his back on her and strode down the hall.

"Where are you going?" she called after him.

"Away from you," he replied over his shoulder. He couldn't think with her standing there crying and his body fighting against his emotions. He couldn't let his feelings erase the facts.

"Tyson, please don't go." Her heels clicked on the tile as she ran after him. "We can talk about this."

He swiveled to face her. "Amber, I can't be thrust into someone else's family."

"I want you to be in our family."

"I don't even know if I want a family!" he shouted.

Silence followed, and he half expected someone from the

wedding party to come out and check on them. But they were too loud to notice.

Amber's voice broke. "I love you."

He shook his head. "I'm sorry for that."

He exited the hotel and made a beeline for his car. He half expected her to come after him, half hoped she would. His throat ached with a child-like need to cry.

Amber was a mom.

That was huge.

She hadn't trusted him with half of who she was.

Tyson backed his car out of the parking lot and peeled out, bitterness coating his mouth. He needed space to think, to be alone. He couldn't be with her right now.

Maybe not ever.

Chapter Eighteen

AMBER

Technically Amber didn't need a ride home now that Deborah had shown up. But she still couldn't believe Tyson had left her. Deborah entertained Raven while Amber tried to be professional and collected as she cleaned up from the wedding. Only after she'd put away the last box did she allow herself to crumple into a chair and drop her head into her hands.

For a moment. She would wait until she got home to fall apart completely.

Deborah parked in front of Amber's apartment, and Amber's hands shook as she unbuckled the seatbelt on Raven's car seat.

"I'm so sorry!" Deborah said. "I wouldn't have come except I wasn't sure what to do!"

"It's not your fault." Amber scooped Raven into her arms, shouldered her purse, and grabbed the car seat with her other hand. "I should've told you about her fevers."

And she hadn't known Tyson would react so vehemently. She had known he didn't want kids, but she thought that maybe when he met Raven . . .

Maybe that would've been true if he had met her in a different way.

She hadn't tried to call him. His abrupt departure was a big enough hint that he didn't want to talk to her.

Deborah helped unload the boxes into the apartment, but Amber just wanted her to leave.

"You still need me tomorrow?" Deborah asked tentatively.

"Yes." Amber nodded.

"I'm so sorry," Deborah said again.

Amber waved her off. "It wasn't your fault."

She paid her and then locked herself in the house, leaning against the front door and sliding to the ground. She felt numb and broken inside, and the aching in her heart was worse than anything she had ever felt before, even when she and Drake broke up. She closed her eyes, allowing a few tears to slide out. But they didn't ease the pain in her heart. *You don't need him*, she told herself. *You have Raven, and your little family is enough.*

Amber read stories to Raven and picked out her clothes for the following week, then fed her dinner and gave her a bath. She put her to bed and threw herself into the deep cleaning before collapsing in a corner and sobbing into her knees.

Who was she kidding? She didn't want to be alone anymore. She wanted Tyson to become a bigger part of her life, to know her daughter. She wanted Raven to know what it was like to have a mom and a dad.

It wasn't until she got to bed that she remembered she still didn't have a car. And tomorrow was the big wedding. The one that could make or break her career. Her heart began racing super fast, and she turned the bedside lamp on. And Tyson—was he so angry at her that he wouldn't bring over the decorations? What about picking up the round tables?

Surely he wouldn't leave her hanging.

She couldn't count on him not to.

Amber called the the first person who came to mind: Mr. Connor. He and Lilly would also be at the wedding, helping with the landscaping.

"Connor Landscaping," an overbearing female voice answered.

Must be Myrtle. "Mrs. Connor, this is Amber Morris, from Tying the Knot. Is Mr. Connor around?" For some reason Amber didn't want to tell Myrtle her request.

"He's outside gathering the plants for the wedding. He should be inside in about half an hour. Would you like me to have him call you?"

But now Amber had another idea, one she felt more comfortable with. "That's all right. I'll see him there."

She hesitated just a moment before calling Lilly.

"Hello?" Lilly answered on the second ring.

"Lilly, hey, it's Amber Morris, the wedding planner?" She tried to summon her professional voice. "I had an incident come up with my car. I know this is kind of weird but . . . do you think you could give me a ride to the wedding tomorrow?"

"Oh. Well, yes, of course. Is everything okay?"

Amber pinched the bridge of her nose. "It's a long story."

"What happened?"

"Let's just summarize by saying it was towed." Why was she telling her this? So much for professional. Maybe she just needed a listening ear. "So I don't have it right now."

"Has it been impounded? Do you want me to take you somewhere to get it?"

Amber exhaled. "That would be great. Then I don't have to

rely on you to take me home again." Amber tried to smile at the phone, but her lips wouldn't turn upward, not even for her own benefit. "I appreciate it."

"Okay. Just tell me what time, and I'll pick you up."

"Is seven all right?" That would give her time to assess the situation at the chapel and reception hall and see what else they needed.

"See you then."

Amber hung up, grateful for Lilly's help. Now she just had to figure out how she was going to fit the rounds into her car and how many trips it would take to get them to the venue.

TYSON

Tyson's first inclination was to go to the bar and get raging drunk, and then find a girl to make him forget all about Amber.

And he knew if he did that, he'd hate himself the next day. And the day after. Maybe even a year later.

So he forced himself to drive home, his hands shaking with anger where he clutched the wheel. He sat in the driveway and took several deep breaths, then he called Connor.

"Hey, Ty," Connor said, answering on the second ring. "What's up?"

"Come over here. Now." Tyson gripped the phone so tight he worried it would break.

"I'm just closing up the store. Should I bring something?"

"You mean, like something to dull the pain? No, thanks. I need to think clearly."

"I'll be there in a second."

Which meant half an hour, if he was closing the store. Tyson couldn't wait that long. He tried Moki next.

"I need an intervention," he said.

"I've got brownies," Moki replied.

"Bring them." Great. Now he sounded like a hormonal teenage girl.

He slammed the car door and went to his room, where he

turned on his Country music and blasted it as loud as he could. May as well act like one too.

Moki knocked on the door and poked his head in. "Brownies. In the kitchen." Just as quickly, he closed the door and left.

Tyson rolled his eyes. So much for listening.

The lyrics changed from vengeful to heartbreak and longing, and Tyson sat down on the edge of the bed. His heart twisted as he realized what he'd done. He'd walked out on Amber. He'd left her stranded at the wedding.

He'd ended them.

His eyes stung and he sucked in several breaths, struggling for control. He bent his head and tugged his hands through his hair. But what was he supposed to do? Every fantasy and imagining of him and Amber, the two of them together, had just been burst by the addition of a third person.

A loud rap came on the closed door. Tyson jerked his head up. He slammed the pause button on the music and yanked open the door.

Connor stood there, eyes wide, an alarmed expression on his face. "What is it? Somebody die? Are you in trouble?"

If only. "It's Amber," Tyson said, and the admission broke him. He rubbed his palms into his eyes, stemming the moisture off.

"Is she okay? What happened?"

"I broke up with her." Tyson exhaled, searching for a measure of calmness in the simple statement.

But Connor's eyes only grew wider. "What?"

"She kept a huge secret from me!" Tyson burst out, banging his fist on the dresser. If anyone understood, it would be Connor. He knew what it was like to have something kept from him.

"Ohhh." Connor drew out the word. He sank into the large chair next to Tyson's bed. "What happened?" he repeated.

"More like, what did I find out?" Tyson growled.

Connor looked at him with an expression of sympathy. "Was she cheating on you?"

It felt like she had been. But no, Amber hadn't lied to him that way. "No. That's not it."

"Then what?"

"She has a daughter."

Now Connor's eyebrows shot up. "She just told you?"

"I just found out. That's why she never wants me over."

Connor exhaled slowly and nodded, his eyes unfocused. Then he looked at Tyson. "But still, she told you, right? She came clean."

He didn't feel like explaining how he'd found out. That wasn't the issue here. Connor was missing it completely. "It's not about coming clean. I'm not her judge. It's that she hid it for so long. That's something that should've come out when we started dating. Or at least, before we got serious."

"But she did tell you. You would be even angrier if she waited six more months."

Would Amber have waited that long? How long could she hide her daughter?

It didn't matter. He knew she hadn't kept the secret to hurt him, but the fact was, he had the right to decide if he wanted to be in a relationship that involved another person. "I don't know, man. It's a lot to take in. I mean, she has a kid, for crying out loud. It's not like having a dog."

"Yeah, that's heavy."

Tyson nodded and studied the carpet. Heavy.

"So . . ." Connor said, his tone cautious, "you don't like her anymore?"

Tyson shot him a look of disdain. "Don't be stupid. I'm crazy about her. But this is kind of a big shock, and I don't know what's worse, finding out I'm expected to be a surrogate father, or that she's kept this from me."

"Did she have reasons?"

"No, other than that she wasn't sure how I would take it and she didn't want to introduce me into her daughter's life and 'cause confusion.'" He quoted the words with his fingers.

"How old is the kid?"

"She's only two. It's not like my presence would've caused some great disruption."

"But you have to admire her thought process. The fact that her daughter came before her relationship with you, that's an admirable trait."

He glared. He should have known Connor would take Amber's side. "I'm not ready to hear all the good things about her," he growled. "You're the one who always says a lie is a lie."

"Hey." Connor threw his hands up in acknowledgment. "I'm not saying to just let it go and pretend like she didn't keep it from you. But maybe give it some time and see if you're willing to accept a little girl into your life."

His words hit home. Was it possible he could learn to live with this new information? Because Connor was right. Everything that made Amber wonderful was still there. Nothing said he had to let go of her.

Nothing except himself.

A sly grin crept across Connor's face. "You'd make an awesome daddy."

"Shut up," Tyson snapped, grabbing the first thing his fingers found and chucking it at Connor. Connor ducked, and the book collided with the door.

"What have you got to eat?" Connor said, his thoughts already elsewhere. "I've been holed up at the store doing schoolwork for the past four hours, and I'm starving."

Tyson grunted. "At least I can always count on you to clean out my fridge." But he clapped Connor on the shoulder as they walked out of the room, grateful for at least one person he could rely on.

Chapter Nineteen

AMBER

No amount of makeup in the morning could hide the fact that Amber had been crying all night. Deborah arrived almost an hour early, and Amber let her change Raven and feed her while Amber got ready.

A gray SUV pulled into the driveway, and a text from Lilly appeared on Amber's phone.

Here.

Amber planted a kiss on Raven's cheek, then headed for the door. As she did so, she realized Raven could show up at any wedding now. She could show up anywhere, actually, because Amber had nothing to hide.

If only she could keep this free feeling and get Tyson back. *Time,* she reminded herself. He wouldn't cut her off forever. He just needed time.

Lilly stayed with Amber until she got her car out of impoundment.

"Are you sure you're okay?" she asked as Amber unlocked the car.

Amber offered a weak smile. "If you could just start setting up the floral arrangements as soon as you get there, I have to get the rounds."

"The rounds?"

"Yes. The tables. This venue doesn't come with them. It's not usually a big deal because we have a contract with a rental company, but I didn't schedule the truck."

"Why not?"

"Well . . . my friend was going to ask Connor if he could use the work truck to pick them up, but something came up, and he can't."

Lilly scanned Amber's face. "If all you need is a truck, my husband has one. Let me just call Nate."

"No, you don't have to—" Amber began, but Lilly was already making the call. She turned her back on Amber and spoke for several minutes before turning to face her.

"Nate said to text him the address and he'll get them. I called Connor to let him know the change of plans."

"Thanks. I need to get a few decorations from the office, then."

By the time Amber got to the chapel with the cut ribbons and a box of other accessories, Nate had delivered the tables. Lilly had the flowers up, and Violet stood nearby with a clipboard, taking notes. Amber ignored her and set the box of decorations in a corner.

Another, much larger box sat beside it, the edges torn from being hauled to various places. Amber frowned and opened it up, curious.

Inside were the arches and candelabras used at the Crescent.

The decorations. Tyson had brought them.

She swiveled around, her heart in her throat, searching the workers for him. But he wasn't here.

Fresh tears filled her eyes. He might hate her, but he hadn't left her hanging.

The wedding, meant to be the biggest in her career, went off without a hitch. The bride and groom looked happy enough to belong to a Disney fairytale, the chapel felt like a glimpse of the tropics, and the guests beamed at them with expressions of adoration and envy. Violet walked over and praised Amber, telling her the feedback she'd gotten from the various weddings was nothing but positive. Amber pasted a smile on her face and nodded, but the words melted together and filled her brain with meaningless jabber. What did all of this success mean if she didn't have Tyson?

She excused herself and pulled out her phone, checking it with an anxious heart.

Nothing from him. He hadn't called, hadn't texted. He knew what this wedding meant to her, and he hadn't even asked how it went.

A rock filled her heart, making it sink to the bottom of her toes. Whatever he had felt for her, it wasn't enough to extend to her daughter. It was clear he didn't want either of them in his life now.

TYSON

It was after ten when Tyson woke up Sunday morning. His eyes ached and his head pounded. His stomach churned when he rolled over, and for a moment he thought he was hung over.

Then he remembered.

Amber.

He sat up in bed and put his head in his hands. It hurt to not talk to her or be near her. They'd grown so close over the past few months.

Which was another reason why her hiding her daughter hurt so much. It was like she didn't trust him, didn't believe in him or their relationship.

But at the same time, he knew who Amber was. She was kind, hard-working, and generous. And protective. She'd shielded Tyson from the feelings of inadequacy his own mother had created, urged him to be something greater. Greater because she believed in him, she saw it in him. Just like a mother would.

Was it any wonder she would try to protect her daughter?

And people made mistakes. That was part of life. Amber had obviously learned from her encounter with the child's father. She deserved Tyson's respect and admiration for making those changes in her life.

He knew all this. But he also knew that now there was a little girl in the picture, and the sense of responsibility that came along with that left him queasy.

No wonder Amber had been so anxious about telling him.

He didn't know if he could do it. He wasn't even sure he wanted kids. But if he wanted Amber, he had to want at least one kid. Because she was already here.

The wedding.

Tyson jerked upright and swore. He was supposed to get the truck and pick up the rounds. This was Amber's big day— the wedding she'd been preparing for for weeks.

He leapt out of bed and grabbed his car keys as he called Connor.

"Ty?" Connor said. "You okay?"

"The truck," Tyson panted, jumping into his car with his pajamas on. That didn't matter. He needed to get the rounds to the wedding. Right now.

"My grandpa's truck?"

"Yes!" Tyson bit back the swear words on the tip of his tongue.

"Never mind it. Lilly called. She said Nate is picking up tables for the wedding so you don't have to."

Tyson paused before leaving the driveway, the adrenaline going out of him. He put the car back into Park, a sinking feeling of acceptance filling his chest.

Amber had known he would fail her.

Maybe that was all he would ever do.

"Thanks, Connor," Tyson said, and he hung up.

At least he'd taken the decorations over the night before.

He took a shower, but it lent no clarity. Then he got breakfast, checked his email, turned on a game. Did his laundry. Vacuumed the house.

The wedding would be over now. Amber had everything she needed there to make it happen perfectly.

But she didn't call. She didn't text him.

Maybe it was for the best. Tyson wasn't even mature enough to handle this obstacle in their relationship. He obviously wasn't ready to handle a kid.

Chapter Twenty

AMBER

A mber stood in front of the mirror and examined her reflection. The short, dark hair bobbed around her shoulders, and her blue eyeshadow matched the blue frames of her glasses. The sharp suit dress she wore gave her a professional, no-nonsense look, but the glasses and bob made her look sassy and friendly.

She'd bought the tailored, gray suit with part of her promotion money. To celebrate and make her feel better about her successes.

For some reason it hadn't worked.

"Mommy?"

The bedroom door opened and Raven popped her head in, followed by Clarissa.

"Come on, Raven," she said, taking her little hand. "Let's get cleaned up before we say hi to Mommy." She looked at Amber. "You look lovely."

"Thank you." Amber knelt down and smothered Raven's face with kisses, smearing lipstick all over the olive skin.

Raven was her success. She needed to be happy with that

and not look for joy anywhere else.

"Good luck," Clarissa said. "Your first day as the boss."

"In name." In reality, nothing had changed. Amber had received a pay increase, but putting on weddings felt normal and natural to her. She had permission to hire an assistant, but she figured she'd just choose from one of the other employees at Tying the Knot. Maybe even Ava, who had good ideas but didn't function as well under pressure. "See you in a few hours."

Her phone rang as Amber walked out to her car, heels clicking smartly across the parking lot. Her heart gave a little jump, like it always did, but she shoved it down. Tyson hadn't called all week. This wedding was at the Crescent hotel, and when Amber checked who would be the manager on duty, she'd been told that there'd been a schedule change and they weren't sure who would be managing the weekend yet.

The message was clear. He'd rearranged his schedule when he saw she was coordinating the wedding. He didn't want to see her or talk to her. And she'd maintained the silence, respecting his need for distance.

She pulled her phone from her purse and froze.

It was Tyson.

Why would he call now? She sent the call to voicemail.

A moment later, a text came through. *Can we talk?*

Amber didn't want to listen to him explain why he wasn't ready to take on the responsibilities of a dad. Why break the silence between them? It was better this way. Just her and her daughter, the way it had been for years, the way it would always be. She'd learned her lesson for good this time. She wouldn't let anyone near her heart.

She dropped the phone back into her purse and climbed into the car.

"We've got one more gluten-free cake," the caterer assured Amber. "I'll send someone back to the bakery for it."

"Thank you," Amber said. Lights strobed across the reception hall, and most of the wedding guests were too busy dancing to pay attention to the food. But the groom's family stood around the table, expecting more cake.

"I really appreciate this," the groom said to Amber as the caterer left. "I know it's more cakes than we ordered."

"It's no problem," Amber said, though she wanted to tell him how lucky he was the caterer had extra and was willing to get one, and that the price of a last-minute cake would be a lot more than the ones he'd preordered. But she kept her smile firmly in place. Let him enjoy his wedding. "I'll make sure the difference gets calculated for your final bill." There. She had to warn him, at least.

"Of course. I'll let my family know more cake is coming."

"Tell them it will be half an hour."

He nodded and gathered his family away.

"Attention, attention," a man said, tapping the mic. Everyone in the room swiveled to look at him, and the DJ paused his boisterous music.

"Before everyone gets too distracted by the dancing and wonderful food," the man said, smiling, "it's time for the toasts. I'll start." He lifted his champaign flute. "To my beautiful little sister."

*Aw*s filled the room, and all eyes turned to the bride, whose cheeks flushed even though she smiled with pleasure.

Bathroom break.

Amber slipped from the room and took the stairwell down to the salon. She stepped into the sterile bathroom and sat down on one of the toilets, then dropped her head into her hands.

Where was the joy she used to get from watching two people put the crowning touch on their romance? Why now did she only feel empty and bitter and envious?

She'd finally gotten the promotion she wanted, and she wasn't even sure she could handle the job anymore.

TYSON

Tyson's emotions had gone through a full spin cycle during the past week. He started Monday a bit depressed, sad he'd lost Amber, but ready to let her go. Ready to move on with his childless life, which was how he preferred it. Even it it meant losing Amber.

By Wednesday he was driving himself nuts missing her. He kept a constant stream of social media and movies playing in the office, on his phone, and at home. Anything to keep him from thinking of her.

Thursday he got a random text from Monica.

Heard you and your girlfriend had a falling out. Get a drink together?

He didn't bother to analyze how she'd heard. He just called her back, glad for the opportunity to move on. He'd been crushing on Monica for years, and if anyone could make him feel like he didn't need Amber, it would be her.

She hung on him, flattered him, and was quite forward with her advances. She made it clear there were no barriers between her and his bed.

So Tyson drove her home and left her there, feeling rotten and dirty for even getting a drink with her.

Amber had ruined him.

By Saturday Tyson couldn't eat. He'd gotten the weekend

off and then he wished for a distraction. He had picked up his phone every other second, wanting to call Amber. It didn't matter anymore how many strings came attached to her. He wanted her, strings and all.

But she didn't contact him either.

Why should that surprise him? What had she done wrong, really? Not that her having a kid was nothing, but Amber hadn't done it to hurt him.

By Sunday morning, he knew he couldn't spend another day without her. He couldn't eat, couldn't sleep, and his nerves were fried.

He gave in. He had to talk to her. Tyson downed an entire can of Pepsi to calm his nerves, but he wouldn't let himself drink anything stronger. He needed to be levelheaded and concise when he spoke to her.

He looked at the phone in his hand, feeling as if he held his heart in his palm. What if she didn't forgive him? What was he supposed to do?

He would face that if it happened.

Tyson press the button for her number. It rang once and then went to voicemail. He swore and shoved his hands through his hair. She hadn't just not picked up: she had declined his call.

He sent off a text. *Can we talk?*

He hesitated just a moment before adding, *I miss you.*

Tyson waited for an hour, curled up on the rug in his living room playing word games on his phone.

Still no response. Fine. He got up, grabbing his car keys. He knew where she lived.

There was an unfamiliar white car parked in front of Amber's apartment. Were they visiting Amber or someone else? Tyson drummed his fingers on the steering wheel, unsure if he should get out or not.

Do it now, he told himself. *Whatever the situation is, face it like a man. You made this mess.*

He got out of the car, closing the door gently behind him. For the first time he understood why Amber had the doorbell taped. He knocked on the door, thoughts of the little girl he barely caught a glimpse of flooding his mind. His stomach knotted. What if she came between him and Amber?

He'd already done a good enough job of that himself.

He swallowed back the doubts and put on a smile as the door opened.

A young woman with her light brown hair pulled up in a ponytail stood there. "Yes?"

Tyson took a step back, caught off guard. He fought off the panicked feeling that Amber had up and left town without telling him. "I was looking for Amber."

The girl's eyes swept over him from head to toe, and then her face lit up. "Are you Tyson?"

"Depends. Do we like Tyson?"

"Amber certainly does." She grabbed his arm and pulled him into the house, then closed the door behind him. "What are you doing here? She said you guys broke up. She's desperately sick over you."

"Is she?" Even Tyson heard the hope in his voice. He glanced around, noting the toys on the ground, the cereal on the couch, and the stuffed animals on the TV stand. No wonder she'd needed a moment to clean up before. "Is she here?"

"Nope. She's working a wedding today. I bet you could catch her. It's at the Crescent Hotel."

The way she said it, Tyson knew she knew he was the hotel manager. Why hadn't he checked the schedule? He would've seen that. "Thanks. I can definitely find her."

He spun to go and nearly toppled over the two-foot-high little girl who had just walked into the kitchen.

Tyson froze. She looked him over, and then walked to the woman and tugged on her pants.

"Clary, who dat?"

The babysitter scooped her in her arms and balanced her on her hip. "That's a friend of your mommy, Raven."

Tyson couldn't take his gaze from her. It was like he was seeing her for the first time. Black curls framed her angelic face, the dark eyes just like Amber's. "Hi."

She leaned her head against Clary's neck and looked at him suspiciously.

Tyson cleared his throat. How should he talk to a two-year-old? "I'm Tyson. What's your name?"

Raven turned her face toward Clary's ear and whispered loudly, "Safe?"

"Yes, he's safe."

That must've been the magic word, because Raven turned her face toward Tyson and give him a shy smile, exactly like her mother's. And in that moment, Tyson melted.

"I'm gonna find your mom. But if your mom says it's okay, maybe I can come back later."

Raven nodded, the curls bouncing up and down against her babysitter's cheek.

Tyson hurried out to his car, a lump in his throat. He hoped Amber would take him back, because now that he knew what he was losing, he couldn't bear the thought.

Tyson parked in front of the hotel and checked his outfit. He wasn't dressed for a wedding, but he hadn't planned on going to one. His jeans and T-shirt would have to do. He probably had a change of clothes in the office, but he rejected that idea. He wasn't approaching her as manager of the hotel, but as her boyfriend. He hoped, anyway.

His nerves took on a life of their own as he approached the reception hall, and he took several deep breaths before pushing the door open and stepping in. He hung out at the back of the wall, unnoticed. A live DJ worked the music, but at the moment a love song played quietly in the background as the groom stood at the mic and praised the attributes of his new bride.

Just like that, Tyson got an idea. But where was Amber? He spotted one of the caterers in a spotless white outfit, standing at attention. Tyson hurried over.

"Excuse me? Do you know where the wedding planner is?"

"Ms. Morris? I don't. She was just here."

Brother. Who might know? He'd have to ask the bride and groom.

The groom had just finished with his speech, and the bride stepped over to him, wrapping her arms around his neck while everyone cheered and clapped. Tyson stepped over to them and waited for them to separate.

"Excuse me," he said, "did you see where the wedding planner went? Amber?" He put on his most disarming smile.

They both shook their heads, but one of the bridesmaids turned around.

"I think she went to the bathroom."

Tyson cleared his throat. "Can you help a guy out? Amber and I were dating, and I screwed up really bad. I need to show her I'm sorry, but I need your help."

The bride and groom looked instantly intrigued, drawing closer.

"Of course, man," the groom said, clapping Tyson on the

shoulder and giving him an understanding look. "Don't let her slip away if she's the one."

Coming from a man recently married, Tyson told himself to take it with a grain of salt. But the words struck a chord.

"Exactly. So. Here's the plan."

Chapter Twenty-One

AMBER

The bathroom door swung open, and Amber heard the rustling of skirts before a voice called, "Amber?"

"Yes?" She lifted her head from her hands, surprised someone would seek her out here. Then she spotted the sparkling yellow shoes under the door and realized it was a bridesmaid. Oh no. Something had gone wrong, and she was in the bathroom having a pity party. How long had she been absent? She pushed open the stall door and hurried out. "So sorry. What is it?"

But the bridesmaid didn't look distraught. Her face was flushed with excitement, a sparkle in her eyes. "You have to come here. Right now." She grabbed Amber's hand and hauled her from the bathroom.

"What? What is it?" Amber asked, completely confused.

The girl didn't answer, just pulled Amber up the stairs and thrust her into the reception hall.

"Oh, there she is." The words echoed from the sound system as the speaker spoke into the mic onstage.

All eyes turned to her, but Amber didn't move.

Tyson stood at the mic, dressed in jeans and a T-shirt as if he'd wandered in off the street. He grinned at her, but Amber could only stare.

"Tyson?" she said. "What are you doing?" She glanced around at the wedding party, but they were looking at her, expectant, nodding, smiling.

He cleared his throat, directing her attention back to him. "I tried to call you, but you didn't answer, so I figured I'd just show up. I hope you don't mind if everyone hears what I have to say."

Her eyes went wide with alarm. "Tyson, come on down from there." Oh, if Violet ever heard about this! "This is someone's wedding."

"Yeah, and they said I could do this."

"I gave him permission!" the groom shouted, and the crowd chuckled.

"No, Tyson—" she began, hurrying toward him, but he talked right over her.

"Amber. You're the most amazing girl I've ever met. From the moment I saw you, I wanted you in my life."

Her breath caught. She stopped in mid-stride, forgetting she meant to get him down, she meant to hush him up.

"You're funny, you're brilliant, and you're selfless. So it shouldn't surprise me that you're also a mom. And—" his voice caught, and he shook his head. "And a good one, at that. I didn't mean for this apology to be public, but, well, you should answer your phone next time."

Again, the crowd tittered, but Amber saw the way they looked at her, with baited breath, anxious to see how this drama would unfold.

"I'm sorry. I'm sorry for my reaction, and if you think I'm

too much of a jerk to give me a second chance, I get it. But if not, I still want you in my life. And your little girl. Really."

Amber moved forward again. "Tyson—"

"Really really. I really want you—"

She reached the stage and took the mic from him, her face hot with embarrassment. "Tyson—"

"Please?" he whispered.

She knew she was the only one who heard the word. But the room was dead silent, the only sound her heart pounding in her ears. Think. She had to think. She'd resigned herself to a single life, to not trying to love someone. Why should she be expected to put herself out there again?

She'd resigned herself.

She didn't want to live in resignation. She wanted to live in expectation, in joy, in happiness.

"Amber," he whispered, his eyes flicking over her face, as if sensing her inner turmoil. "I love you. Please don't make me go through life without you."

TYSON

"**P**lease don't make me go through life without you."
It sounded like a cheesy line, but Tyson's breathe
caught after he spoke the words. His heart was on
his sleeve, in his throat. But if she didn't forgive him now, he
wasn't gonna let this go. He wouldn't let her walk out of his
life even if she wanted to.

"I could sing for you," he said, trying a smile, though his
pulse thumped in his throat. "Cause I've had the—"

"Stop talking," she said, putting her hand to his lips.

He swallowed. "Amber, I—"

"Hush!" She glanced around at the crowd of people and
then back at Tyson, a torn expression on her face.

He'd made a scene and embarrassed both of them. But he
just wanted her to listen to him.

"Can I—"

"Tyson!" Amber grabbed his face and kissed him hard,
which brought a chorus of jubilant whoops from the watching
crowd. "Why can't you stop talking?" she whispered, still
holding his face.

Tyson inhaled her scent and closed his eyes, pressing his
forehead to hers. He'd feared he'd never touch those lips again
with his own. "Did you only kiss me because everyone's
watching?"

"Yes. And no." She grabbed his hand and pulled him away from the mic. "Just give us a minute, guys," she said to anyone near enough to hear her. Then she tugged him out of the reception hall.

Now he'd done it. Tyson could just imagine the talking-to he was about to get. Amber didn't say a word as she pulled him out of the hotel and down the walkway by the gazebo.

"Amber," he said, finally breaking the silence, "can I talk now?"

She let go of him and moved under the gazebo, wrapping her arms around herself and keeping her back to him. Tyson approached hesitantly, knowing he'd wounded this woman more than she could let on in front of a crowd of people. He stepped up behind her and touched the back of her arm gingerly. When she didn't react, he launched into the words that had been swimming through his mind for days.

"Sorry if I embarrassed you back there, but I had to get your attention. You weren't answering my calls."

"You called once," she said, her words tight.

"And you ignored my texts."

"One text."

"Two."

Her head shifted toward him, though her hair still blocked her face. "I only saw one."

He let out a careful breath. She was listening, at least. "I sent two. This morning. Asking if we could talk. And telling you I miss you."

"I didn't hear from you all week," she whispered.

He felt another pang of guilt. Sure, he hadn't heard from her either, but he was the one who had instigated their break up. "I was scared. Terrified, really. Because I love you, and suddenly loving you meant loving someone else also . . . and that was . . ."

"Unwanted."

"Unexpected," he corrected. "It caught me off guard."

"When we talked about kids, you said you didn't want any surprises. Anything unexpected."

"Amber." He used his hold on her forearm to swivel her. She turned reluctantly, dipping her head so her hair fell over her face. Tears sparkled in her eyes, on her face. He swept her hair back with his hand and used his thumb to wipe the tears on her cheeks. "We were speaking hypothetically. It's a little unfair. It's like asking your boyfriend how he feels about kids when what you mean to say is, 'I'm pregnant and will you support me?' and judging him because he doesn't give the answer you want to hear when he doesn't know."

"I've had that conversation too," she whispered. "Turns out his girlfriend being pregnant didn't mean anything."

Idiot. Tyson had set himself up for that one. "I'm not that dude." He held her shoulders, forcing her to maintain eye contact. "I would never have abandoned you if I'd gotten you pregnant."

"You don't know that."

"Sure, I do. Let's get you pregnant and I'll prove it."

She laughed, finally, and some of the tension eased out of her shoulders. "Tyson."

"I went to your house this morning." He softened his tone. "I met Raven."

She looked at him, her eyes widening. "You did?"

"I went looking for you. And I met her. I don't want to mess up her life, but I would love to be a part of it. If you'll let me —" Tyson choked on his words, surprised at the emotion that welled in his throat and stung his eyes. "I know I have to earn your trust. But I want to be there for you. Always. And I want to be there for her. Be everything her dad—no, her biological father—hasn't been."

Amber burst into tears, and Tyson froze, afraid he'd said all the wrong things. But then Amber threw her arms around his neck and sobbed into his shoulder.

"You just said," she sobbed, "everything I've always dreamed someone would say to me someday. That there would be some man willing to be not just a companion for me, but a father for Raven."

He wrapped his arms around her body, holding her close.

"But I was afraid to hope. If her own father didn't want to be in her life, how could I expect someone else to step up?"

"I don't know anything about parenting," Tyson said, speaking over her head.

"Me neither."

"I know what I don't want to do."

"That's a start."

"So." He pulled back to study her. "Can we give this a go?"

Amber's eyes flicked over his face. "With Raven?"

He shrugged. "When you feel it's right. When you're ready. But I can tell you this, Amber. I'm not going anywhere."

She slipped her hand in his. "I'm starting to believe you."

Chapter Twenty-Two

AMBER

This time, Amber was there when Raven met Tyson. They went back to her apartment after the wedding, and Amber gathered Raven and Tyson together in the living room.

"Raven," she said, holding her in her lap on the couch, "This is Tyson. He's Mommy's friend."

"Very good friend," Clarissa said, earning a dark look from Amber.

"Hewo," Raven said, peering at him beneath her eyelashes.

"Sometimes she's shy with new people," Amber said.

"That's okay." Tyson leaned forward on the couch, elbows on his knees, his posture belying his anxiety. "I'd like to be your friend, too, Raven." He glanced at Amber and back at Raven, and she wished she could know his thoughts. "Can I?"

"Um. Otay." Raven hopped from Amber's lap and went to her box of toys in the corner. She pulled out a teddy bear and a doll. "For you." She handed him the bear, then walked her doll across the carpet, singing in a high-pitched voice.

Tyson looked at Amber again, and she nodded at him. He

sat down on the floor, an uncertain expression on his face, and trailed his stuffed bear after the dolly.

"I guess I'll go," Clarissa said, her voice singsong. "Just call me when you need me."

"I will. Thank you." Amber didn't take her eyes from Tyson and Raven. She swallowed against the way her heart pounded in her throat. Was this a good idea? What if Raven grew attached to him?

Mr. Bear rode around on the wooden train until Ms. Doll got hungry, then Raven dropped all the toys and ran into the kitchen. Amber stood up to follow her.

"Thanks for playing with her. Now you've met Raven."

Tyson put the toys back in the box, then turned around and squished Amber to him in a hug. "I'm so sorry, Amber. I know why you didn't tell me, and I don't blame you at all. But I love you." His mouth found hers, claiming it greedily, his hands cupping the sides of her face. "And I love her. Because she's yours."

Amber returned his kisses, her chest filling with warmth, heat building behind her eyes as his words healed the wounds of her heart and tore down the walls she'd spent the past few days putting up. She clung to him, her hands clenching his back, holding on as he kissed her cheek and her nose and then took her glasses off and kissed her eyes. She laughed also.

"I love you. I love you too."

Tyson squeezed her closer and whispered in her ear, "And guess what? I got into law school."

Amber pushed away and stared at him, her eyes flicking over his face to see if he was joking. "You did? When?"

He grinned. "A few weeks ago. You're the only person I've told."

She caught her breath and pressed a hand to the base of her

neck, clutching the angel charm of her necklace. Her heart pounded with sudden trepidation. "Where?"

He pulled her back to him. "Fayetteville. I start next fall."

She leaned her head against his chest and closed her eyes in relief. Turned out she didn't want him going anywhere after all. "Congratulations, Tyson. I'm so happy for you."

He squeezed her hand. "For us. For Raven. Because from now on, it's the three of us." He tipped her chin up, catching her eyes. "If you want."

"I do."

Forever. For always.

Don't miss Connor's story in the next Eureka in Love series!

Connor wonders when it will be his turn to find someone he can love with all his heart instead of constantly second-guess. But what he doesn't realize is that falling in love is the easy part.

Chapter 1

Luce

"Yeah, it's great, Dad. I appreciate you finding me a place."

Luce held the door open with one hand, balancing the heavy box on her hip while cradling the cell phone between her ear and her shoulder. Crumbling stone steps led the way from the concrete sidewalk exterior into the faded brown condo. Even with the curtains pulled back from all the windows, the wood paneling kept the interior dim and enclosed. Glass fixtures enclosed the living room light, adding an orange-ish glare to the galley kitchen next to it.

"I wish you would let me come and help you," her father said, his normally stern voice hinting at something almost like concern.

Not that Luce fell for that. She knew her dad still blamed her for the divorce. "I'm almost done. I've got the last box in my arms. And you've done enough." She fought hard to keep the bitter edge out of her words, not wanting to bring up the sore subject of her new career path. "I'll call you if I need anything."

"Let me know how your first day at the clinic goes tomorrow."

"Sure. Talk to you later."

The call disconnected, and Luce gave an aggravated sigh, letting the phone slide from her shoulder to the floor. She stepped over it and inhaled deeply, trying to get a sense for her new home, but mostly she smelled must and moth balls, a scent that reminded her unpleasantly of her grandma's house. She dropped the heavy box onto the giant rug in the middle of the living room that the previous inhabitant hadn't felt the need to take with them.

Yay. An old condo badly in need of a remodel. This was

what she inherited from her broken marriage.

Melodee came in behind her with her arms full of blankets. "Careful with that box!" she said. "It might have some of your pottery in it."

Luce's lip twisted. She never wanted to look at another clay vase or glazed plate again. She kept quiet, though, because she knew Melodee already worried about Luce's mental health. She didn't think the anger at her pottery was "normal."

Like normal was even a real thing.

Melodee pressed a hand against her lower back, the growing bulge of her belly made more evident by the pose. "Was that Dad?" Her long brown hair with reddish highlights, the same color as Luce's, fell in waves across her shoulders. Though four years older, Melodee was shorter by several inches, and there was no hiding her pregnancy.

"Yeah. He just wanted to make sure I got in okay." Luce had left her dad's house in Springdale an hour earlier, just as anxious to get away from his parental care as she was to reestablish herself as as single, independent woman.

Melodee looked around the room at the yellow light fixture and the dated kitchen behind her. "Nice place. First time seeing it?"

"I came up with Dad to look at places a few months ago. But I told him to just pick one." She could be in a one-room hut in Africa, as long as she was away from Brian.

The desire to redefine herself, to discover her identity as an individual, loomed over Luce, feeding her hands with a nervous energy. She tapped the pads of her fingers against her thumbs. Without meaning to, her eyes turned toward the box labeled "wheel." She could take a glob of clay right now, set up her wheel, get it spinning and spinning while her hands caressed and molded it . . .

Shake it off. She exhaled slowly. "I'm actually looking forward to being by myself."

Melodee favored her with a smile. "I'm sure you are. But dinner's on me, okay? We'll go walk the strip."

The strip? Luce bit back a laugh. The idea of comparing the mile-long shopping center in Eureka Springs with the miles of entertainment available in Vegas was hilarious at best, insulting at worst. "Sure, that would be great. I'll be hungry."

"You know I will be."

Luce waved goodbye and then surveyed the boxes in the living room.

"A new start," she breathed, her eyes locking on the one box she had hauled around for the past six months without opening. She knew the contents by heart: the blanket Brian had given her when they went to the drive-through movie; the stuffed animal he slept with when he was eight years old; the jersey he let her borrow for their first football game.

Silly things, and just things; yet they reminded her of a time when she and Brian were happy. When she had been excited about spending the rest of her life with him.

If only she had known then about his addiction, his need to put the things most precious to him on the line so he could get an adrenaline rush.

Luce didn't need to go through the box. She already knew what to do with it. Squatting down and grabbing it with both hands, she carried it outside and tossed it into the dumpster.

***

Melodee stopped by a few hours later. The weather was unseasonably cool for late September, and Luce threw on a jacket before heading outside. It would be easier for the two of them to walk twenty minutes to the strip than to take the car and try to find parking downtown. The parking spaces were for the tourists, people willing to pay five dollars because they didn't have any other choice.

"Did you get all unpacked?" Melodee asked as they started down the sidewalk.

Trees covered in lush leaves crowded the walkway, long branches reaching out over their heads and creating a barrier from the wind. Luce glanced up and stared at the different shapes and sizes, the deep dark green color. That shade of green didn't exist in Vegas.

Something unfurled within her, as if her own budding tree was trying to grow in her chest.

"Mostly," Luce answered, turning her gaze back to the sidewalk before she lost her footing. The steep inclines in Eureka could catch even the experienced natives off guard. "It's not like there was much. I just threw a few things in my car and left." She'd only been married a year, after all, just enough time for Luce to lose everything.

Melodee shot her a sideways glance. She shoved her hands into her jean pockets, thrusting her body backward to balance her weight while they walked down the hill. "Have you talked to Brian?"

Luce mimicked her sister's pose as the steep downgrade threatened to make her topple. "No. Not since the court settlement." She'd spent the last year existing in her dad's basement while she went to school in Bentonville, a town thirty minutes away. By throwing her life into her studies, she'd completed a two-year degree in just one.

"Does he know where you are?"

Luce lifted a shoulder. "I hope not. I didn't tell him." And she'd changed her number.

They turned a corner onto Spring Street, and the first shops came into view. Luce's spirits rose at the sight of the little eclectic buildings full of designer jewelry and crafts, funky artifacts, and vintage items. The narrow street continued its curving path, but the colorful stores and waving awnings beckoned them forward. All of the buildings had two or three levels, constructed as they were into the hillside. They staggered beside each other at different heights like stair steps, decades old and built in a Western style, all right angles and brick. Music spilled out of the open bars and restaurants along with the crowds, groups of people dressed in comfortable jeans and casual shirts leaning against the railings and chatting.

Luce let out a soft sigh as a few more leaves unfurled in her chest.

"Sure was nice of Dad to help you score your job at the clinic," her sister said, a hint of something in her voice.

Luce frowned. "Yeah, it was nice of him." Their father was the CEO of the local chain of hospitals and clinics. He'd urged her to finish her nursing degree—urged? More like forced—, and it hadn't taken much for him to secure her a job as an RN. "My life choices have been a big disappointment to him."

"The past few years have been hard on him."

"Hard on him? Try hard on me."

Melodee's hand fluttered in a nervous gesture. "Well, there's no question about that. But—"

Whatever she was trying to say was cut short when they rounded the corner and Melodee smacked into a man coming up the opposite direction, his head turned toward the people with him instead of facing forward.

"Watch it!" Luce gasped, dropping her purse as she reached for her sister.

"I'm so sorry," he said, grasping Melodee's elbows and helping her straighten herself. "I really should slow down going around corners."

"It's okay. I'm fine. Like I keep telling everyone, I'm not fragile."

All Luce could see of their perpetrator was a square jawline and some stubble from at least two-days worth of beard growth. Something about the shape of his jaw reminded her of Brian, and her defenses flared. "You should pay more attention. You could've hurt her."

He turned toward her, the chagrin showing in his light brown eyes. His olive-toned skin evidenced the time he spent in the Arkansas outdoors, and dark brown hair with a slight wave fell back across his forehead, and any similarity to Brian, with his fair, freckled skin and light hair, faded away. "You're absolutely right." And then his eyebrows lifted. "Luce? Is that you?"

Luce squinted, recognizing some familiar features on this man-face. "Connor?" Even as she said it, she knew she had to be mistaken. It couldn't be the same person.

His face split into a smile, revealing a dimple on either side. "Yeah!"

Her mind flashed back to the boy with an acne problem and glasses. "I tutored you in English, right?"

His smile shifted more to the shy grin she remembered. "Turns out I'm more of a math guy."

She'd felt bad for him then, the quiet boy who never spoke to her, not even in tutoring sessions. Apparently he'd outgrown that phase, and his friends snickered and whispered to each other behind him, their eyes on Luce.

Luce glanced at them and her face warmed, embarrassed to have them scrutinizing her. "Hi," she said, inexplicably flustered. "Nice to see you again." He still stood there, gaze intent on her, and she found herself unable to break eye contact. Luce rolled her wrist. "Well, my sister and I are going to get going."

Connor looked behind him at his two friends who stood waiting. "Yeah, of course. I'm on my way back to my mom's store anyway. The one on the corner?"

He pointed, so Luce looked, obligingly, but she couldn't tell which store was his. "Oh."

"I work there," he said, as if he couldn't tell she wanted to leave. "So do you live here now?"

His eyes on her did something weird to her stomach, and Luce forced herself to look away. She hooked her arm through her sister's and pulled her down the sidewalk. "Yes. Bye, Connor."

"Wait!" He bent and grabbed her purse from the sidewalk, then held it out to her. "You almost left this."

Luce tried to keep her stern expression, but she couldn't help giving him a tiny smile as she took it. "Thank you."

At least Melodee had the decency to wait until they had gone a full block before she brought Connor up. "Seriously? You should have been all over that. He was super hot. And a friend of yours from high school!"

"He's not a friend from high school. He's just someone I knew. Six years ago."

"Maybe you should get to know him better."

Connor *had* come into himself quite nicely, a far cry from the scrawny kid who sat silently in the back of the classroom. "I just got out of an ugly marriage."

"A year ago. You can't keep thinking the male species is all evil."

Luce set her jaw, her eyes burning. "Brian was perfect. Remember? He was funny, friendly, the perfect son-in-law. That's why Dad still likes him more than me."

Melodee fell silent. Luce knew her sister had nothing to counter that, but it didn't feel like a victory.

Melodee took her hand. "I'm sorry. But hey, let's look on the bright side. We're at the fudge shop."

Luce exhaled. "You know my weakness."

Connor

Luce O'Neil. Connor could not even believe it.

Luce O'Neil, here in Eureka Springs.

He hadn't seen her since high school, and it wasn't as if he'd talked to her then. But he'd noticed her. And even though she'd been nothing but a tutor, she'd always been kind. His secret little crush grew to quite an obsession by the end of their senior year. She had the same long auburn hair, light brown eyes, upturned nose and freckles on her face, but her eyes hadn't glittered quite as brightly. But what did he expect? None of them were carefree teenagers anymore.

And there he'd stood, blabbering like a stupid idiot. Like she cared where his mom's store was.

"Connor." Ty nudged him. "We're going back to your shop, right?"

Behind Ty, Moki snickered. "I think he got bushwhacked."

Connor glanced around and realized he'd walked right past the antique shop. "Oh, yeah, sorry."

"Sure, she was pretty." Ty opened the door and held it while they walked in. He deposited his soda can on the glass counter top and leaned against it. "But seemed like more than that to you."

Connor gave the store a quick once-over, surprised to see it empty and unlocked. His mom had been here when he left. He shoved Tyson off the glass counter and handed him the soda, then wiped the counter down with a cloth, removing the ring of water. He'd known Ty for six years and Moki for three, and they knew him about as well as he knew himself. "We went to high school together."

"And?" Ty pressed, his blond eyebrow almost invisible as it arched into his strawberry blond hair. Moki leaned in also, his braided black hair and olive skin a direct contrast to Ty.

Connor stopped shining the glass and bent toward them. "Okay, yeah, I had a big crush on her. What of it? I had a crush on half the girls in school. At some point or another." Which wasn't exactly true.

"What happened to her?"

"Beats me." Connor shrugged. "Last I heard, she dumped her boyfriend and ran off to a big city."

"And now she's back." Ty scrutinized Connor.

"Now she's back," Connor agreed. "So? I have a girlfriend, and we're happy."

"Sometimes," Moki said.

Ty snorted. "The fire's gone out of that one."

Connor didn't respond. He turned around and organized the antique porcelain teacups on their matching saucers, wishing once again his mom would let him fill the shop with something newer. Nobody wanted antiques anymore. They wanted modern, sleek, cutting edge. Original. He looked over at his shelf, the one he filled with items from his various travels. She tolerated it, but if he tried to sneak in more than that, she'd remind him of Granny's vision for the store.

"Oh, look at the time!" Tyson said, clapping Moki on the shoulder. "Closing time. We're out of here."

"What?" Connor said. "You don't want to stay and help me clean up?" He hauled another rag out from under the counter.

"Nah." Ty grinned broadly. "Meet us at the Rowdy Beaver

tonight. Bring Regina, Amber will be there too. We'll watch the game."

Yeah, but Ty's girlfriend Amber followed him around with the kind of devotion that made Connor's stomach hurt with envy. Regina liked him, but was she devoted? "We'll see if she wants to."

Connor raised a hand in goodbye and began the tedious work of closing the shop. Not hard to count the money in the till today, since only a handful of customers had come in. A little less than three hundred dollars. It would have to do. Hopefully the next day would bring in more.

He picked up the mail under the counter and sorted through it, looking for one thing: the foreign trading post. He sat on the stool and hunched over the magazine when he found it, flipping through pages with a pen in his hand, circling items he thought would sell well. The Christmas retail season would be upon them in a month, and now was the time to get in the decor.

"Hello!"

The back door pushed open at the same time that Connor's mom poked her head inside. She smiled at him, her natural hair color long hidden by boxes of blond dye.

"Oh!" She giggled as she stepped inside.

Which meant that—

Sure enough, her boyfriend Dave came in behind her, poking her teasingly.

"Oh, Dave," she said, turning and slipping her arms around his neck, "stop that."

Gross. Connor grabbed the bank deposit envelope. "Hey, glad you're here. I was just leaving. You guys can finish closing up." It was his mom's store, after all, and he shouldn't have to babysit it.

"I've got places to be," Dave said, throwing up his hands. "I'll meet you at the winery, Jess?"

"Of course," his mom purred, leaning into him.

Connor averted his eyes from the inevitable kiss, but the noises were unmistakable.

Finally Dave walked out, and his mom plopped down on the stool next to him with a sigh.

"The winery? Again?" Connor said. "Seems you're doing that a lot lately."

"It's what Dave likes to do, honey." She smiled at him patronizingly as if he were a child who didn't understand why dads had to work. "So I like it, too."

"But you don't like it."

"Maybe I'm developing a taste for it."

Connor pressed his lips together before the argument went full force again. There was no point. With the last boyfriend, it had been black and white movies, the one before that, golfing, the one before that, antique cars. He had to admit his mom had become very well-rounded in all of these relationships, but she was never herself.

Not that she knew who she was. She'd been trying to define that person ever since his dad walked out.

"Where were you, anyway? You were supposed to be watching the store," he said, closing the register.

"Dave picked me up an hour ago. I knew you'd stop by before closing."

"So you just left?" Why did he feel more responsible for this place than she did?

"I locked the door," she sniffed.

"No, you didn't."

"Didn't I?" She looked suitably chastised.

"I'm out of here." He handed her the keys. "Don't stay out

too late."

"You don't stay out too late." She took the keys and eyed him, the giggly girlfriend quickly replaced by the concerned mother. "Going out with Regina?"

"Maybe."

She softened her voice. "You two been rocky lately?"

"Yeah."

She patted his arm. "I want to see you happy and tied down."

He grunted. Did those two things even go together? Yeah, Regina was nice, but he couldn't really see himself tied down to her. "We're doing fine, Mom."

"What time will you be home?"

"What time will *you* be home?" he returned, shouldering his messenger bag. "I won't be late. I have a few assignments I gotta finish up before the weekend." Connor had gotten his bachelor's degree in art history from the University of Arkansas a year and a half ago, but somehow it didn't prove to be worth much in the job market. Since he didn't plan on being stuck to his mom's/grandma's/great-grandmother's antique shop for the rest of his life, he was taking online classes to get a master's in business management.

The odd thing was, he felt a certain affection for the shop. If his mom would just let him change it. . . . But he knew he'd have to break away and open his own store if he wanted his vision to become a reality.

"A race, then. We'll see who gets home first."

"Me," Connor said, unable to hold back the grin. He hurried to the door to show his mom he meant business.

"Not tonight!" she shouted after him.

"You're opening tomorrow!" he called back.

The back door to the shop closed behind him, and Connor

descended the stairs to Mountain Street. His calves tightened as he started up the steep incline to the parking lot, but he was used to it, having lived in Eureka all his life. The backs of shops greeted him, all with steps leading up to them from the street below. Nothing was straight or level in this town. As a kid, it infuriated him not to be able to skateboard or ride his bike around the sharp curves. Now, he couldn't imagine trading this charm and style for anything.

How hard would it be to find a girl who felt the same way?

Probably not Luce. She'd run off to the big city the moment school got out. Couldn't wait to get away from the small-town scene. He shook his head. Why was he even thinking about her?

***

Connor spent a few hours at home trying to get homework done and study for his Friday exams. But his mind kept wandering back to Luce. Her long reddish brown hair had fallen in soft curls down her back, though her expression had been rather steely. He'd apparently really offended her when he bumped into her pregnant sister.

He checked the time. Nearly eight. Regina would've gotten off work hours ago. Why hadn't she called? Picking up his phone, he dialed her number.

She answered on the fourth ring. "Hello?" she whispered, her voice groggy, as if she'd been sleeping. He pictured her with her white-blond hair tucked into a high ponytail, black eyeliner ringing her eyes. But she was off work now, so maybe she'd let her hair down.

The thought didn't excite him the way it had a few weeks ago.

"Hey, Gee," he said. "You okay?"

"Oh, yeah." She cleared her throat. "You studying like

crazy?"

"I was." He rolled his pencil across the notebook. "Moki and Ty invited me out for drinks. I told them I'd think about it. Did you want to go out tonight? Amber will be there."

"You're so sweet." She gave a cough. "I think maybe a patient got me sick. My throat kind of hurts."

"Ah." That explained the husky note to her voice. "I'm so sorry. Should I come over?"

"No, I don't want to give it to you. Besides, aren't you going to ace those exams this time?"

He chuckled slightly. "That's the plan." Last time he'd scraped by with a low B. He definitely didn't want his master's education to be sub-par.

"I'll leave you to it, then. We'll talk tomorrow."

Connor hung up and sent out a quick message to Tyson. If Regina didn't feel up to coming, he didn't really need to, either. Besides, she was right. He needed to score high this time.

DON'T MISS ANY OF THE BOOKS IN THE EUREKA IN LOVE SERIES!

EUREKA IN LOVE SERIES

Chocolate KISSES

RIVER FORD

EUREKA IN LOVE SERIES

Forgetting YOU

HILLARY ANN SPERRY

EUREKA IN LOVE SERIES

Landscape LOVE

RIVER FORD

EUREKA IN LOVE SERIES

Teacher's CRUSH

RIVER FORD

EUREKA IN LOVE SERIES

Shades of RAVEN

TAMARA HART HEINER

EUREKA IN LOVE SERIES

After THE FALL

TAMARA HART HEINER

Sign up to be one of Tamara's Readers

And get sneak peeks, exclusive content and sales, and juicy gossip about me, my characters, and upcoming stories! Never miss a new release!

Text TREADER to 33777!

Loved this book? Please consider leaving a review! When I have 50 reviews, I'll start working on the next book!

About the Author

Tamara Hart Heiner is a mom, wife, baker, editor, and author. She currently lives in Arkansas with her husband, four children, a dog, and a bird. She would love to add a macaw and a sugar glider to the family. She's the author of several young adult suspense series (*Perilous, Goddess of Fate, Kellam High*) the *Cassandra Jones* saga, and a nonfiction book about the Joplin Tornado, *Tornado Warning*. She's new to romance, and she'd love to hear your thoughts!

Connect with Tamara online!
Twitter: https://twitter.com/tamaraheiner
Facebook: https://www.facebook.com/author.tamara.heiner
blog: http://www.tamarahartheiner.blogspot.com
website: http://www.tamarahartheiner.com
Thank you for reading!

www.ingramcontent.com/pod-product-compliance
Lightning Source LLC
Chambersburg PA
CBHW050021180626
46810CB00002B/522